master's mates

PETER CORRIS is known as the 'Godfather' of Australian crime fiction through his Cliff Hardy detective stories. He has written in many other areas, including a co-authored autobiography of the late Professor Fred Hollows, a history of boxing in Australia, spy novels, historical novels and a collection of short stories revolving around the game of golf. He is presently at work on the twenty-seventh Cliff Hardy book.

PETER CORRIS

master's mates

A CLIFF HARDY NOVEL

ALLEN&UNWIN

For help in Noumea, thanks to Denise and Dennis Fisher, Philippe Boisserand and Pierre Faessel. Thanks also to John Hertzberg, Cathryn Hunter, Jo Jarrah and Jean Bedford.

First published in 2003

Copyright © Peter Corris 2003

Allen & Unwin
83 Alexander Street
Crows Nest NSW 2065
Australia
Phone: (61 2) 8425 0100
Fax: (61 2) 9906 2218
Email: info@allenandunwin.com
Web: www.allenandunwin.com

National Library of Australia
Cataloguing-in-Publication entry:

Corris, Peter, 1942– .
    Master's mates: a Cliff Hardy novel.

    ISBN 1 74114 136 2.

    1. Hardy, Cliff (Fictitious character)—Fiction. 2. Private investigators—Fiction. I. Title.

A823.3

Set in 12/14 pt Adobe Garamond by Midland Typesetters
Printed in Australia by McPherson's Printing Group

10 9 8 7 6 5 4 3 2 1

For Abi, Mark and Louie

1

'**D**ID my name mean anything to you when we spoke on the phone, Mr Hardy?'

Her name was Lorraine Master and she was in my Darlinghurst office at 2 pm, as arranged, right on time.

'I've known a few Lorraines and some Masters, but no one putting them together.'

'Put together' described her pretty well and that was probably why the remark occurred to me. She was tall with broad shoulders and then everything tapered down. Her eyes, skin and hair were dark and her teeth and tailored suit were snowy white. She had high cheekbones and a broad mouth over a strong chin. She smelt vaguely of some flower, one of the thousands I couldn't name, and the perfume was working well against the dust and damp spores that flavoured my office. She exuded confidence, but with it there was a note of strain, a tension.

'I'm Stewart Master's wife, Stewart Henry Master, that is.'

'Ah,' I said. 'That can't be easy. What did he get, ten years?'

'Twelve with ten to serve minimum on account of his record. But he's innocent.'

Master had been convicted of attempting to import a sizeable quantity of heroin from New Caledonia. He was a career criminal with a long list of prosecutions and quite a few convictions.

'Stewart never had anything to do with drugs,' she said. 'Never! He didn't use them and he didn't sell them. He's a health freak, a body builder.'

He's in the right place then, I thought. All the time in the world to work on his lats and pecs and everything else.

She was sitting very straight in the client's chair, which isn't that easy to do because it has hard spots. That's deliberate. A private detective doesn't want clients to get too comfortable. They might decide that it's just good to talk, get it off the chest, and go on their way. I was on a much better chair behind my desk with things to fiddle with. I fiddled while I spoke.

'As I remember, Mrs Master, they found the heroin in the false bottom of a suitcase that held your husband's things.'

'That's so, with presents for the children and me in the case too.'

'Well . . .'

'It was planted. That wasn't Stewart's suitcase.'

'I'm sorry. I didn't follow the trial closely. He—'

'You just took in the charge and the conviction, like everyone else.' Her smile was thin with no humour in it.

'I was going to say he must've claimed the bag.'

'It was identical to his, but it was switched.'

I was fiddling with a ballpoint pen and just managed to stop myself from clicking it on and off. I put it down. 'Where, by whom and why?'

'That's what I want you to find out and I'll pay you very well to do it.'

'That's encouraging. But just say I could do it, what good would it do?'

'Then whoever's responsible could be convicted and Stewart'd be let go.'

She was somewhere in her thirties, well educated and confident. I couldn't help wondering how she'd hooked up with a crim like Master. She wore discreet makeup, fashionable clothes and muted accessories. She seemed the kind of person who expected things to turn out well for her, but minute cracks were showing. The last statement was too simple and she knew it. She shook her head and her glossy, shoulder length hair danced.

'I need help,' she said. 'The kids need their father, *I* need him.'

That impressed me. Not a rave against fate or the lawyers or the cops. Good word, help. I needed it myself often enough to be glad to give it if I could. *If.* It didn't sound likely.

'Let's look at it,' I said. 'The customs guys couldn't do the switch, could they?'

'No.'

'Baggage handlers wouldn't have the time.'

She'd been sitting with her hands still in her lap. Now she clenched her fists and tapped them together. 'Not at the Sydney end, no. It must've happened in New Caledonia and that's where I want you to go.'

It was September, two weeks after the media blitz on the anniversary of the attack on the twin towers and the story was still running, although there was a weird segue to the threat posed by Iraq to the 'freedom loving people' of the world. The day was cloudy and dull but the light in the room seemed to lift as she said New Caledonia. I had visions of palm trees and blue lagoons and snorkelling under a tropic sky. I looked at my hands, a bit pale after winter, scarred from fights and accidents, and I shivered although it wasn't cold. I'm a summer type, greedy for the sun, and now maybe I wouldn't have to wait for it.

'New Caledonia,' I said, just to be saying it.

'You know where it is?'

'Vaguely,' I said. 'You turn right at Townsville.'

'Rockhampton actually, but near enough.'

The correction reined me in a little. If I didn't really know where the place was, how likely was it that I'd be any use there? 'I don't speak French.'

She laughed, showing those strong white clackers and the thought crossed my mind that being shut away from her must be bloody hard for Master. 'Neither does Stewart or any of his mates. There's a whole gang of them over there and one of them, or a couple, must've set Stewart up.'

'Why?'

She shrugged. 'Thieves fall out.'

'You're frank about him.'

'Stewart's a con artist, a fraud merchant, a thief, but he's not violent and he doesn't deal in drugs. He . . . he mostly takes advantage of people who're trying to take advantage of him.'

'What was he doing in New Caledonia?'

'Property deal. Legitimate.'

'It could've gone wrong. He could've been sucked into something he couldn't control. It happens.'

'Not to Stewart. Too smart.'

'I seem to recall convictions.'

'A long time ago when he was careless.'

Did she mean before he met me, I wondered. I picked up the pen and dropped it again. 'You want me to go over there, link up with these mates, whoever they are, and get one of them to own up to . . .'

'It's not quite as raw as that.' She reached down for the big leather bag she'd put beside the chair. 'I've got some letters he wrote me, with names and places.' She took out several airmail envelopes secured with a rubber band. 'And also . . .' She dropped the letters on the desk and hauled up a big ring binder. 'A transcript of the trial and I've spoken to Stewart's lawyer about getting you access to visit him. I don't expect you to take this on without checking up on us and doing some preparation.'

'You were pretty sure of me, Mrs Master, but I don't know how realistic you are. Your husband's . . . what? In his early thirties? And a body builder. I suppose his mates are the same vintage and shark hunters, windsurfers or whatever. I'm not in the first flush of youth and I can't take my AK47 to New Caledonia. How d'you think I should proceed?'

'By bribery. I'm offering you a hundred thousand dollars to spend on getting what I want.'

2

B Y mutual agreement we didn't sign a contract there and then. I undertook to read the letters and the trial transcript and ask around about Master while his wife made arrangements for having the money available in New Caledonia. She made it clear that if I refused the job she'd look for someone else, which tapped straight into my competitive instinct.

'You can keep the transcript,' she said, 'but not the letters. I only brought the originals to show you they're genuine. You don't have a photocopier?'

I waved my hand. 'As you see. There's one in William Street close by.'

'Low overhead.'

'That's right. Do you mind telling me how come you've got a hundred grand going spare?'

She stood up to a full 180 centimetres in medium heels. 'Yes, I do mind. But I'll tell you this—it's not Stewart's ill-gotten gains.'

I put the transcript in a drawer, she picked up the bundle of letters and her bag and we went out and down the stairs into St Peters Lane. Her looks and the white suit turned heads as we made our way to the motor showroom where they let me use the copier. I wondered why she wore something like that on a dull day with rain threatening. Maybe she liked turning heads.

I copied the letters and we shook hands. We exchanged cards. Hers said she was a business consultant and carried an office phone number, a mobile number and an email address. I hadn't got around to putting the email address on mine. She left the showroom. At a guess, her BMW—a Merc maybe—was in a nearby car park.

Chris Rowley, a salesman I sometimes have a drink with and who's never quite given up on the idea of selling me one of their Saabs, wandered over and gave a low whistle.

'Client?'

'Yep. Maybe.'

'Looks well heeled. Are you on a good earner, Cliff?'

'Could be, with travel.'

'Ah, time to replace that clapped-out Falcon with something more reliable?'

'Overseas travel.'

'Good luck to you. Don't forget to pay for the copies.'

I did some calculations as I walked back to the office. If I took the job on it'd be a few weeks at least before I could expect to show any results or admit failure. At four hundred dollars a day plus expenses the cost would rack up pretty high, and New Caledonia was bound to be expensive. Everything French is. But funds didn't seem to be a problem for our Lorraine. I realised that she'd told me nothing about herself. I was intrigued and it was a fair bet that was part of her plan.

. . .

In the office I tidied up a few things I'd left hanging—sent off a few emails, a couple of invoices and paid some bills. I realised that I was clearing the decks for the Master matter. No contract, no retainer—not best business practice, but then I've never been known for best practice at business or anything else.

I copied Lorraine Master's phone numbers and email address into my notebook and looked at the sheets of photocopy paper. There were six letters spread out over a month or so. The handwriting was a big, loopy scrawl, easy enough to read. Immature perhaps. For some reason, maybe because I wanted to get a more objective view of Master before encountering him directly, I put off reading the letters. But I was still detecting. Because you have to see both sides to get the full message on an airmail letter, I had the Masters' address—Double Bay, and a house not an apartment. Nice. And another thing—the letters probably didn't contain any passionate endearments or improper suggestions or she wouldn't have handed them over so readily. Of course there could be others, she might have culled them, but six letters in four weeks wasn't bad for a bloke.

I put the photocopies and the transcript in a shopping bag and locked up the office. As I went down the stairs I caught traces of Lorraine Master's perfume and I wondered about the condition of the marriage. A hundred thousand was a lot to spend on someone. Was it an investment? I was going to have to do some digging. I remember a historian telling Phillip Adams on 'Late Night Live' that although it was nice to have letters it was better to have them to and from, otherwise you only had part of the picture. In a way, this game is like being a historian or an archaeologist. The whole story isn't on the surface.

Early spring in Sydney isn't much different from late winter, which can be pretty much the same as autumn. In the hour or so since I'd been on the street the wind had picked up and was colder. New Caledonia beckoned all the more strongly. I had to walk quite a few blocks before I reached the car and I was glad to get inside. It still held some of the earlier warmth of the day. I drove home to Glebe looking forward to parking a big scotch by the computer and searching through newspaper files on the web for Stewie. Well, looking forward to the scotch.

When I got inside the phone was ringing. I let the machine pick it up.

'Mr Hardy, this is Bryce O'Connor. I'm Mrs Master's legal representative and—'

Quick work, Lorraine. I picked up. 'This is Hardy.'

'Good. I gather you want to visit Stewart Master?'

'Well, yes, I—'

'Would tomorrow suit?'

'Tomorrow! What's the rush?'

'Mrs Master is anxious to get things moving.'

'Just bear with me a minute, Mr O'Connor. You say you're Mrs Master's lawyer?'

'Correct.'

'Did you defend Master?'

'I did. Unsuccessfully.'

'This is probably a silly question to ask, but d'you think Master's innocent?'

'Usually I wouldn't answer such a question, but yes, I do. This was entirely out of character for him.'

Marvellous how some people can be such accurate judges of character. I should be so cluey. 'Did you recommend this course of action to her?'

'No.'

'Why not?'

'Not to put too fine a point upon it, I don't have a high opinion of private detectives. Now, my time is valuable, Mr Hardy. Would a 10.30 am appointment at Avonlea prison suit you?'

From the tone of your voice I'd rather it was you inside to be visited than Stewie Master, mate, I thought, but I agreed and he hung up first to save spending another valuable half second. I dropped the receiver and listened to two other calls that didn't amount to anything important and went to get the scotch. I like a brisk pace generally, but this was starting to feel like a flat out sprint. Lorraine Master had a no doubt high-price lawyer and a medium-price private detective jumping through hoops. Good going.

I poured the drink and took it upstairs to where I keep the computer in the spare bedroom. I made a mental note to check on Bryce O'Connor because I felt sure I'd have further dealings with him, and on Lorraine Master, naturally. Then I began my trawl for the dope on Stewart Master. In the old days this would have meant visits to newspapers or libraries and fiddling about with microfilms or, still worse, microfiche. Now it's a comfort-of-your-own-home job with a drink to hand. In one way I like it, in another I don't. There was something about getting out, rubbing up against people to get what you wanted, that felt good, gave you a feel for things.

The subscription to the *Sydney Morning Herald* database is another overhead, but a valuable one. I turned up the paper's coverage of the Master trial and read through the reports carefully. I also studied the photographs and saw that the lensmen hadn't missed an opportunity to get pictures of Lorraine. She turned up every day in a variety of outfits.

Nothing flashy, all designed to show, firstly, how mature and respectable she was and, secondly, how attractive. Would a man smuggle drugs, risk gaol, risk losing me? her appearance seemed to say.

It didn't do any good. Master, born in Melbourne, arriving in Sydney in his twenties, was a career criminal, the amount of heroin was large and he'd been 'uncooperative' with the police. O'Connor, giving him his due, had stressed Master's non-involvement with drugs and his relatively clean record in recent times. A family man, happily married, a sportsman.

The clincher was Master's fingerprints on one of the plastic bags containing the dope. O'Connor argued that these could have post-dated the discovery of the bags but two customs officials swore that Master hadn't touched the bags. O'Connor tried the Mandy Rice-Davies argument—'Well, they would say that, wouldn't they?'—but it didn't work. An election wasn't far off and law and order toughness was the watchword. Justice Mary Pappas wasn't looking to get her sentences reviewed for softness and she hit Stewie with twelve big ones.

As far as I could judge, Bryce O'Connor QC had performed adequately under extreme difficulties. The surprise was the inept contribution from Master himself. For a silver-tongued conman with an imposing physical presence he came across as limp and unconvincing, insisting that the heroin had been planted. After the report on the sentence there was no further mention of Master. All this had happened nearly six weeks before and I scribbled a couple of questions as I finished the last article and the scotch simultaneously. Why no appeal? And why the quickness of the trial—a few weeks only after the arrest?

My eyes were hurting. I logged off and went downstairs to scramble some eggs and drink some wine. In a moment of weakness I'd bought a case of cheap chardonnay advertised by leaflet in the letterbox. The wine was okay but the offers kept coming by snail mail and email until I was sick of the sight of them. Also, having a whole case of wine ready to hand didn't help my periodic attempts at moderation.

As I ate, I thought about prisons. I'd been briefly on remand in Long Bay many years before and had visited people there, but not recently. I'd served a short sentence at Berrima for obstructing the course of justice a while back and that was about it for personal experience. I'd heard that things had changed in the prison system but I didn't know anything about the changes and nothing about Avonlea. Another web search.

I rinsed the saucepan, plate, knife and fork and glass, ate an apple and brewed a pot of coffee. I sorted through the mail I'd brought in and dumped most of it in the bin. I poured the coffee and was about to go up for another computer session when the door bell rang. I wandered down the passage with the mug in my hand and opened the door without turning on the porch light. Didn't want to look too welcoming. A large figure loomed up and shoved me aside as it bullocked its way inside.

'Hey!' I yelped, partly from surprise and partly because hot coffee had hit my hand.

I spun around. My intruder had taken a few strides inside and was leaning against the wall, panting hard.

'What does she want?' he shouted.

I don't take to being brushed aside and scalded. I put the mug down, kicked the door shut, and moved up on him prepared to pay him back. He was a surprise packet. He levered himself off the wall and came at me swinging. I caught a strong smell of alcohol and sweat as his punch missed and his suit jacket swung open. I dropped my shoulder and hit him hard in the sternum. I felt it bend. His flailing hands fell away and I caught him with a solid left to the ribs. All the breath went out of him and he sagged back against the wall, knees buckled. He was a sitting duck and I didn't have the heart to hit him again. Besides, he was very drunk and I didn't want him throwing up on me.

He was wobbling, close to tears. He wore a dark suit, blue shirt and red tie like a banker or a politician, except that the tie knot had slipped down below where I'd hit him. I grabbed a handful of shirt and tie and eased him along to the stairs. He didn't resist and I dumped him on the third bottom stair the way you handle a bag of clothes destined for St Vinnie's. He reached for the banister and winced. A good rib shot hurts. He was pale and having trouble catching his breath.

'I'm sorry,' he said.

'You fucking should be. Hang on. I'll get you some water.'

I recovered the mug and swilled down the remainder of the coffee. In the kitchen I filled a big glass with water and took a quick swig of scotch.

'Here you go.'

No response.

I reached the stairs and found that he'd stretched out with his legs splayed forward and his top half resting comfortably. He was out cold.

I wasn't copping that. I took careful aim and splashed the water in his face. His eyes opened, he coughed and spluttered and tried to go back to sleep. He was as tall as me and heavier by ten kilos. Younger by at least ten years. Heavy. I hauled him up and dragged him into the kitchen. His head bounced off the doorjamb but just hard enough to trigger some adrenaline, not to knock him out. I placed him so that his head hung over the sink. The first retch started around his ankles and shook him like a dog coming out of water. He vomited hard, drew in a laboured wheezing breath and did it again. And a third time. The kitchen smelled as if I'd dropped a bottle of whisky on the tiled floor, a thing I'd never do. I wet a tea towel and put it in his twitching hand. Still bending over, he wiped his face, dry-retched a couple of times and turned slowly around to face me.

The light in the passage and over the stairs is dim, the kitchen light is a harsh fluorescent. It bleached him and gave him a greenish tinge. Dark stubble showed through the pale, stretched skin; his eyes were bloodshot and pouchy. Some vomit had splashed up onto his shirt. The paper towel dispenser had busted long ago, but I keep a roll in the same spot. I tore off a couple of sheets.

'Clean yourself up and then you're going to tell me what this's all about.'

He nodded and turned on the tap. When he'd finished he ran water in the sink until it was cleanish. Good manners. The coffee sat in a beaker on a hotplate. I poured a mug for myself and held the beaker up enquiringly. He shuddered and shook his head. I handed him a glass and he filled it with water and drank.

'You better keep that down,' I said.

'I will.'

'How's the chest and ribs?'

'Sore.'

'Good. Who are you and what're you doing here?'

'My name's Tony Spears. I'm Lorrie's . . . Lorraine's husband.'

'Her husband's in gaol.'

He managed a thin smile, then thought better of it and set his mouth against his rising gorge. He gulped and his Adam's apple moved in his thick neck. 'That bastard's her third husband,' he mumbled. 'I'm her first.'

3

TONY Spears told me that he'd been married to Lorraine Van Hewlen, as she was, for two years seven years ago.

'I met her at university,' he said. 'We were both doing economics and I was a year ahead. I helped her because she was struggling. I did pretty well and got a job in an investment firm. We got married at the beginning of her final year. I drilled her hard and she did brilliantly, topped everything. She got a job in a merchant bank and dropped me the next day. Two years, but it was more like a tutorship than a marriage, except that . . . except that I was in love with her and I still am.'

Poor bastard, I thought. 'What about husband number two?'

'Bloke in the bank. Fat, bald, rich as shit. She took him for a packet. She'd made all sorts of connections under his wing and she set up on her own. She's flying high.'

'But married to a career crim.'

'Doesn't seem to have done her any harm, professionally.' He'd regained some colour and was pulling himself together. He asked to use the toilet and when he came back he'd spruced himself up a bit and accepted a mug of black coffee. He sipped the brew and gave a despairing sigh.

'I don't understand it. A man like Master. Okay, she used me and Lance Robbins, but him . . .'

'Some women go for men like that. They marry them in gaol. Want to have their babies, smuggle out sperm. Look at that woman with the helicopter.'

'Is Lorrie trying to help Master escape?'

I laughed. 'Do I look like an idiot to you?'

'No, I do. What's she up to?'

'I can't tell you. And what's it to you anyway?'

'I told you. I still care about her. I thought once Master was out of the way . . .'

'Mate, she's gone. She mentioned kids.'

'Yeah, one by Robbins and one by Master. She was on the pill when we were together and she still made me use condoms.'

'So what happened today?'

'I . . . I snapped, I guess. I saw her go to your office. Then I followed you back here and—'

'You *saw* her? Are you stalking her?'

'I suppose so.'

'You're sick.'

'I know. Look, I'm sorry I burst in like that. Can I help in any way with what you're doing for Lorrie?'

'No.'

'I could charge you with assault.'

'You were the trespasser, and no one's going to say that a bit of a shoulder jolt and a punch in the ribs is excessive force.'

I got up and took the empty mug from his hand. I pulled him to his feet by his tie and walked him out of the room and down the passage to the door. He struggled at the very end but I had a firm grip. I opened the door, pushed him through and slammed it.

I watched him through the peephole. He reached to ring the buzzer and thought better of it. He stood there for a minute or so and then squared his shoulders and marched down the path to the gate. He fumbled for the catch and swore before he managed to get the gate open. Was he sober enough to drive? I really didn't care. I spiked another mug of coffee with a good slug of scotch and went back upstairs to the computer.

Nine o'clock the next morning found me on the road to the Avonlea complex, forty odd kilometres from the CBD. My computer searches the night before had told me that Bryce O'Connor was a member of a city firm specialising in criminal law. He was a partner along with a McPherson and a Williams—all the Celtic bases nicely covered. The website for Lorraine Master's firm, LP Consultants, told me very little and didn't allay my scepticism. About investment consultants I tend to take my cue from a Woody Allen line in *A Midsummer Night's Sex Comedy*: 'I'm an investment adviser. I advise people how to invest their money until it's all gone.' Maybe it's just because I've never had any to invest. A couple of stray thoughts crossed my mind as I drove. Was the money Lorraine Master spoke about giving me to splash around in New Caledonia actually hers? And could I believe her about Stewart Master and drugs? What about body builders and steroids, and one thing leading to another?

At least I knew what to expect at Avonlea. Or not quite. The website had said that the Avonlea Correctional Centre housed mainly young offenders between the ages of eighteen and twenty-five. Stewart Master's age had been variously given as thirty and thirty-one. Hard to see him squeezing in, except for that 'mainly'.

For an inner-city liver the Western Highway is a dreary stretch that seems to take you further and further away from what Sydney is all about. A narrow view. Prejudiced. I tried to resist it as I made the drive to Parramatta and beyond, reflecting that this was now the demographic heart of Sydney and an area that held almost as much history as Sydney Cove. Almost. Trouble was, the turn-off to Sunnyholt Road towards Blacktown and Avonlea only reinforced the pessimistic impressions. How could so many car salesmen, mechanics and auto electricians make a living? Surely all these second-hand cars couldn't be sold and, if so, what happened to them in the long run?

It was hard to arrive at Avonlea in an optimistic frame of mind and I wondered how the lawyers, like O'Connor, coped. How did they feel when they saw the acres of housing estates, one dwelling much the same as another, without privacy or individuality, springing up and being occupied in what was essentially a wasteland? Shut the eyes, enjoy the air conditioning and look forward to lunch. The wooden frames were sprouting like mushrooms on the approach to the prison, as if people couldn't wait to live there. But the completed houses, fenceless, with struggling gardens and not a tree in sight, told another story. You couldn't get to anywhere else from here unless you had a car. If you didn't and you were old, you probably stayed put; if you were young, you probably 'borrowed' one.

The Avonlea Correctional Centre announced itself in big letters on a brick pillar one side of a security gate. The pillar on the other side said 'Young Offenders Program'. I looked the place over from the car park before I approached the gate. At this distance the sprawl of buildings behind a series of fences looked like a cross between a cash-strapped provincial university and a Christian holiday camp. The sky was overcast, keeping the temperature down, and there was a mild breeze. In high summer, low lying as it was, it'd bake like an oven, and in winter the winds would cut you to the bone.

I showed some ID and was buzzed through the first gate. Then I went through another gate and was divested of my mobile phone, 'Hot item in here, mate,' the guard said. He put the phone in a locker and handed me the key. No charge. Then this friendly type ushered me along a one hundred metre path further into the prison. We went past an exercise yard where a few inmates were walking, talking and smoking. I wouldn't have called it exercising. The yard was divided into sections and I had a feeling that the dark skins and the lighter skins were being kept apart.

I showed the pass I'd been given and was admitted to another area where my escort left me. Up a set of steps and into a sterile room divided up into glassed-in cubicles. I submitted my pass and the name of the inmate I wished to see and a guard said he'd be paged. I waited, looking back to the exercise yard where nothing physical seemed to be taking place.

'Cubicle four, sir,' the guard in charge announced.

I took a seat in cubicle four. I wasn't the only visitor. At least three of the other cubicles were occupied, including the one next to me. An intense conversation was being carried on between a youngish woman, a lawyer to judge by the papers she was passing across, and an even younger inmate dressed in the bottle green uniform—tracksuit pants, T-shirt.

A buzzer sounded, a door slid open and a man stepped out and headed towards the cubicle. Almost everything about him surprised me. He wore the greens as if they'd been his own choice. He wasn't tall, 175 centimetres at most, but he looked as if that was all the height he needed. Lorraine Master had told me he was a body builder, but he had none of the misshapen exaggerations that often go with that tag— the excessive muscularity behind the sloping shoulders, the wide arm carry and the crotch-splitting thighs. This man was all of a compact, well-developed piece. I ruled out steroids. And he looked young. Younger than Lorraine. Almost young enough to be here.

'Stewart Master.'

We shook.

'Cliff Hardy.'

'How is she?'

I studied him. Long term prisoners get a certain look in their eyes, as if they can't quite focus on the here and now. As if the past, the present and the immediate future are too painful to think about. Master had nothing of that. He was intensely aware of the moment, engaged in it as an actor.

I shook my head. 'I don't know her well enough to say.'

He nodded. 'You better fucking keep it that way.'

4

'WHEN did you last see your wife?' I asked Master.
    'Six weeks ago.'
'Speak to her on the phone?'
'Just as long, or longer.'
'How come?'
'That's how I want it.'
'Why?'
'None of your fucking business.'
'She's making it my business.'
'She's wasting her money then.'
'You mean you're guilty.'
'No, I mean the only thing worth spending money on is a lawyer—get the sentence reduced, get parole, get me moved somewhere else. That sort of thing.'
'You knew your wife sent me. How?'
'She told O'Connor. He advised her against it but she went ahead. That's what she's like. She does what she thinks best. Usually it is.'
'Like marrying you?'
'Fuck you.' He started to get up.
I said: 'Your mates and your playground—Reg Penny,

Gabriel Rosito, Rory McCloud, Jarrod Montefiore, Le Saint Hubert, the Salon de Fun.'

He sat down with a bump. The guard by the door had moved as Master had half risen, now he settled back down. 'Where did you get all that?'

'From your wife. Where else? Did one of them set you up?'

He shrugged. 'One of 'em. All of 'em. Who knows?'

'I'm going there to ask around. Are you going to help me?'

'No.'

'Don't you want to get out of here?'

'I'll get out.'

'In ten years.'

'I told you, we're working on that.'

'I can't fathom you, Master. You don't look stupid. Don't tell me you're thinking of escaping.'

'Don't *you* be stupid. If I was, would I tell you?'

'Why did you agree to see me?'

'I just wanted to see what sort of a dickhead you were and to warn you to keep your distance from Lorrie.'

I studied him and thought I saw something behind the tough exterior. It's a look you see in lonely people, a neediness behind the defensive shell. I pushed my chair back. 'Well, you've done that. You can rot in here for all I care, but I'll take the job and see if I can give satisfaction.'

He seemed about to say something but thought better of it. He signalled to the guard, got up and walked away without a backward glance. I sat stunned. Some pretty heavy discussions were going on in some of the other cubicles and I was tempted to listen to find out if these contacts were going as unsatisfactorily as mine. But the voices fused and I couldn't make any sense of what was being said. The guard signalled for me to leave and I did, retracing my steps with another escort who had nothing to say. I was grateful for that.

I couldn't say I liked Stewart Master but I was certainly interested in him. I was intrigued by his indifference, even hostility, to what I'd been hired to do. You'd have thought a man in his position would be clasping at straws. His relationship with his wife was unusual evidently, but marriage is an unusual institution. I recalled a remark a friend had made: golf is like marriage and marriage is like golf—they're *designed* to make you unhappy. I was interested enough to have decided to take the job but I needed to see Lorraine Master again to clear a few things up; among them, Tony Spears.

I drove back to Darlinghurst and went up to the office. I pulled out a contract form and dialled LP Consultancy's number. The phone was answered by a well-modulated female voice.

'LP Consultancy. This is Fiona. How may I help you?'

'My name's Hardy. Is Mrs Master available?'

'She's very busy, Mr Hardy.'

Her first husband was an obsessed stalker, her third was behind bars and razor wire and she hadn't seen him for weeks, I had questions and wasn't in a mood to be put off by Fiona, well modulated or not. 'Tell her I'll be there in ten minutes.'

The office was in a tasteful commercial block in a tasteful street in a tasteful suburb. Something, probably in poor taste, had been knocked down to provide car parking space for the tenants. In Double Bay you can buy practically anything you want at approximately twice the price you pay anywhere else. As a guarantee of quality, that's an unreliable measure but a lot of people go for it. I had no doubt it applied to business consulting in spades. Money likes to be around money.

She was in a black suit today. Lorraine Master, that is, not Fiona, who was so waif-like she scarcely made an impression. The office was nicely done out in Swedish wood, vases, flowers, pictures—all those things my office lacks. Her computer was state-of-the-art and it looked like she'd got as close to the paperless office as was possible. She held out her hand across the desk—two rings on the hand on the surface of the desk just where they should be.

'Mr Hardy, I gather you've been to see Stewart.'

I shook her hand. 'Word gets around. Hope I didn't intimidate Fiona.'

'Fiona's a state high-diving champion. I doubt you intimidated her. Sit down.'

I sat. Her computer was emitting a soft buzz and lights were flashing on her telephone console but she ignored them. I had her full attention. 'Your husband couldn't give a toss about what you propose.'

'I know.'

'Do you know why?'

'He has faith in Bryce O'Connor.'

'You don't?'

She shrugged. 'So far the track record's not good.'

'Why wasn't there an appeal?'

'No grounds.'

'There's always grounds.'

'That's what I said. They disagreed.'

'They?'

'Stewart and O'Connor.'

'Don't you find that odd?'

'I do, yes. But so what? You can't force a person to appeal if they don't want to.'

The Samuel Goldwyn line sprang to my mind: 'If the people won't go you can't stop them.' What she was saying seemed to have something of the same logic. She was sitting perfectly still behind the desk with her dark eyes fixed unwaveringly on my face. There was something very unsettling about her, and attractive, very attractive. 'I'm puzzled by your husband's attitude to you,' I said.

'What do you mean?'

'His refusal to see you.'

She sighed and the force field around her lessened a fraction. 'He doesn't want any distractions. He's focused on legal manoeuvres and surviving inside the gaol, physically and . . . psychically.'

'Psychically?'

'Stewart's got a very strong spiritual side. It's giving him strength, but it takes strength to maintain it.'

Bullshit, I thought. I sat back in the chair and she read me accurately.

'You think that's nonsense, don't you? So do I. But that's what he says and I think he means it. Anything that helps him to stay . . . strong . . . is fine with me. Who are we to say different?'

She was manipulative. That's okay, so am I, so are we all. She was good at it, too—enlisting me as it were. I almost pulled out the contract there and then, but not quite. 'You seem to have a lot of pull with the lawyer. I'd like to meet him, but QCs are hard to get to see.'

'I'll arrange it.' She tapped a few keys on the computer. 'When?'

'ASAP.'

'This means you've accepted the commission?'

I nodded and took the contract from my blazer pocket and passed it over. She must have topped her speed reading course. She took in the contents rapidly, signed and took a cheque book from a drawer.

I spoke again before she wrote the cheque, timing it so as to rattle her. 'There's one more thing I'm not clear about.'

Gold pen poised, she said, 'What's that?'

'Tony Spears.'

It didn't rattle her. She carried on writing. 'Already? I knew you'd run into him sooner or later, but not this soon.' She flashed me a smile as she handed over the cheque. 'I hope you didn't hurt him.'

Boot on the other foot but I tried not to show it. I took the cheque, folded it and tucked it away along with the contract. 'You'll get a proper accounting.'

She leaned back in the chair. 'Tell me about Tony.'

I told her.

'He's a fool. I've taken out restraining orders against him time and time again. But he persists.'

'Master . . .'

'Beat him up. It didn't stop him. When I broke up with Lance I may have offered Tony some encouragement—in his own mind at least. He's a pest. I'm sorry he bothered you.'

'Not really much bother. I just wondered. Is it possible he could have anything to do with setting your husband up?'

She let out a burst of laughter. The first reaction I'd seen from her that wasn't under total control. 'Tony? No, he's harmless.'

And that, I guessed, was about the worst thing Lorraine Master could say about a man. I told her I'd leave for Noumea in a couple of days and she said she'd let me know about the money. We shook hands again. I walked out with some of her money but nothing else she hadn't wanted me to have.

I took a longer look at Fiona in the outer office and I saw that she wasn't quite as waif-like as I'd thought. Slender, but like a gymnast, which is what a diver is in my book. Behind hers there was another desk which had been empty when I came in. A man was sitting at it now operating a computer. He glanced at me without interest and went back to his screen. He was young, dark and good-looking.

I was in Broadway on the way back to Glebe when my mobile rang. I made the turn into Glebe Point Road, pulled over and answered. Fiona told me that an appointment had been made for me with Bryce O'Connor for 4 pm that afternoon. I thanked her, drove to the bank, deposited Lorraine's cheque and bought a thousand dollars worth of Amex traveller's cheques. I had a late lunch at the café beside the Valhalla theatre and made some notes from memory on my conversations with Master and his wife. I wondered why I hadn't told Master I'd read his letters to his wife. Maybe I was worried about disturbing him spiritually.

The travel agency did me a deal on a return flight to Noumea with four days at the Sunrise Surf hotel thrown in. I booked the flight for two days ahead and put the charge on my American Express card. Lorraine was going to be facing a pretty hefty bill, but, from the look of the office, Fiona, the young screen jockey and herself, that wasn't going to be much of a problem.

With time to kill, I wandered into Gleebooks' second-hand store and bought a tourist guide to New Caledonia and a French phrase book. My high school French was a long way behind me and wasn't too flash anyway. I remembered the eye doctor, Frank Harkness, who I'd once bodyguarded, saying you only needed to know two things in a foreign language—'Take off all your clothes and lie down,' and 'My friend will pay.' I doubted I could get by on that.

'Going travelling, Cliff?' Sam Ross, who works in the shop and puts books aside for me, asked.

'Yeah.'

'D'you know what things cost in New Caledonia?'

I shook my head.

'You'll get a shock. Checked the exchange rate?'

'Fair go. I'll only be eating and drinking, I'm not planning to buy a beach.'

'You won't be drinking much, I'll tell you that.'

'Good. You know me, Sam—occasional social. That's what I put on life insurance forms.'

'Have a good time.'

'I'll try.' As I said it, I realised that I wasn't approaching the case with a fully professional attitude. Did I really expect to sort out who'd planted heroin on Stewart Henry Master? No. But I didn't think the Masters were playing straight with me either, so I'd go along and see what panned out. Or not.

For a fairly law-abiding type, I have extensive experience of lawyers. Fortunately, they get to employ me more than I have to employ them. As a species, I prefer lawyers to doctors and I rate them well above politicians, at least until a lawyer becomes a politician, which too many of them do. There was no danger of Bryce O'Connor becoming a politician. Nowadays the breed has to look reasonably good in a single breasted suit and O'Connor would never make it. Too many bulges in the wrong places. He looked like a front row forward gone to seed, and, as his teeth were obviously capped, maybe he had been. He was balding, bull-necked and red-faced but he had shrewd little green eyes. They fixed on me as soon as I was ushered into his handsome office and they didn't like what they saw. We didn't shake hands.

'I don't see the need for this meeting, Hardy.'

I sat down in a comfortable leather chair without being invited. 'The thing is, what you don't see don't matter.'

'Are you trying to be funny?'

'Yes,' I said. 'I'm trying to be funny to get over all this mutual hostility so that we can talk some sense.'

His office had all the fixings—crammed bookshelves, filing cabinets, vast teak desk, computer, phone/fax and a medium-sized conference table. Degrees and other certificates on the walls. He glanced around as if to assure himself that he belonged here and then let go a smile with the too-perfect teeth.

'I was told you were an arsehole, but a good arsehole to have on your side. I'm a bit the same.'

'Who told you that?'

'I'm too much of an arsehole to tell you.'

'You recommended me? I thought you held a low opinion of PEAs.'

'I do.' He pointed at the table where four sets of papers were laid out. 'I've got a meeting in twenty minutes. Talk.'

'What are Stewart Master's chances of getting his sentence reduced?'

'Slim.'

'Why isn't he backing his wife's attempt to find out who set him up?'

It was warm in the room and I was sweating inside my blazer. O'Connor's suit was of some lightweight material that probably breathed, as the ads say. He shrugged and the suiting moved smoothly on his burly frame. 'He's not the sort of man to put any faith in women.'

'In women generally, or in his wife in particular?'

Another shrug.

'She says she's prepared to spend a lot of money to clear her husband. A six figure amount.'

'Your question?'

'Is she good for it?'

'She certainly is. She trebled her divorce settlement in a matter of months and has significant investments and a list of high-profile clients.'

'Why didn't you appeal, if money's no object?'

'Have you read the trial transcript?'

'Not yet.'

'You must. I've practised criminal law for twenty-five years and Master's was the most remarkable trial I've ever been involved in.'

5

Wᴴᴬᵀ he said made me wish I had read the transcript. I'd been saving it for flight reading. I looked at my watch. Time was short and O'Connor was the type and in the profession to mean what he said about it. 'Please explain.'

'Have you sat through many trials, Hardy?'

'A few, yes.'

'Raggedy affairs, aren't they?'

A surprising thing for a QC to say but I was in agreement. 'They can be.'

'Not this one. I've never seen a better prepared, better marshalled, better argued case. The Crown had everything sewn up tight—witnesses word perfect, evidence spotlessly presented, technical stuff exactly right.'

I held up a hand. 'Hold it. What does that mean?'

'You'll see when you read the transcript. Scrupulous chemical analysis of the heroin, precise evaluation of its quality and . . . financial potential. That was crucial. The anticipated returns were off the graph. Just for bringing in a couple of packets of powder. The jury . . . shit—' he broke off as his composure sagged momentarily. 'The jury couldn't wait to convict this bastard who'd tried to book himself into paradise.'

He was good, very good. I felt sure then that Bryce O'Connor would have done all he could for Master and found it not enough. That answered one of my questions, although it threw up quite a lot of others. His statement had wrung him out a bit and left him unhappy, not in the best condition for his meeting. I eased up out of my chair and gave him a respectful nod.

'Thanks for your time, Mr O'Connor.'

The pain and discomfiture were still working in him. 'Get fucked,' he said.

'Last thing. Who was the prosecutor at Master's trial?'

'John L'Estrange.'

'Might be worth having a chat to him.'

'Good luck.'

'Meaning?'

'You'll find him in Holland, at the Hague. He got some sort of job in the War Crimes Tribunal.'

'When was this?'

'Soon after he got ten to twelve for Stewart Master.'

Trying to be a good citizen, I'd taken a bus into the city. As I left the Martin Place building that housed O'Connor's firm I felt in need of exercise and decided to walk home to Glebe. Sometimes I've found that walking, if I can strike a good rhythm, can help with thinking. Not always, sometimes I just get tired. I strolled down to Goulburn Street and bought take-away chicken and salty fish from the Super Bowl, my favourite Chinese restaurant. More Asian faces than Anglo-Celt but Australian accents all around. Up through Ultimo into Glebe. A few years ago all the streets were littered with overflowing skips as the terraces were renovated or pulled down for facsimiles to go up in their place. There's less of that now as the area settles down into its gentrified state. There are still ungentrified patches though, like my house.

I had a quick beer in the Toxteth, bought a bottle of red and went home to watch the TV news, eat and study the trial transcript, maybe get my tongue around a few French phrases. 'Good evening, are you alone?' 'May I join you?' 'Would you like to . . .?'

The news consisted of more posturing about Iraq and I turned it off before the program finished. I put the take-away in the microwave and went upstairs to fetch the transcript. I poured some wine and sat down at the kitchen bench. The door bell rang. Not again, I thought, but it was a courier with the card that would allow me to tap the hundred thou.

Trial transcripts make frustrating reading. There's too much legal quibbling holding up the action, the same ground is gone over and over again and there's a kind of sterility coming off the pages because you don't get a sense of the audience. Throw in the spectators and bit players and you can get the sort of stuff that works so well in plays and films and novels. Without it, dullsville. The newspaper reports were still fresh in my memory and this helped to flesh things out a little. Now that I'd met O'Connor I could see him in the role and there had been artists' sketches of John L'Estrange, whose name hadn't stuck with me, and of the judge. And of course, although she didn't participate, Lorraine Master was there in my imagination.

Another frustration arises from the questions that come to your mind as you read. You want to be there to ask the witnesses questions that seem important to you but apparently didn't to the learned counsel.

As I turned the couple of hundred pages, skipping the dull stuff, I thought I could see what O'Connor meant. John L'Estrange had presented the case against Master in a straightforward manner that seemed to say, Look, no tricks. This is all above board. Judge for yourself. Likewise, the judge's summing up had been scrupulously fair, without frills or flourishes. Reading between the lines, you could get a sense of her law-and-order agenda as reported in the newspaper, but there was nothing the defence could point to as untoward.

I closed the binder and sat back with only one phrase coming to mind: a very neat package. I'd put my notebook beside the transcript but when I'd finished reading I only had three names written down—Salvatore Verdi, Colin Baxter and Detective Senior Sergeant Karl Knopf. Verdi and Baxter were the customs agents who'd inspected Master's bags and detained him. Knopf was the forensic examiner who'd analysed the heroin and done tests on the packaging. There was no reason why any of them would be willing to talk to me and possibly nothing to be gained. But you never know. Ten to twelve was a heavy sentence and if any one of them was surprised by what resulted, they might have started thinking . . . Besides, I had two days before my flight and had already talked to the principals, so it was time to try the supporting cast.

As I finished the wine and poured another glass, I realised that I hadn't turned the microwave on. I do that. I sometimes take out mugs of coffee and find them stone cold. I heated the food and ate it slowly, enjoying it and the wine and regretting that there was no one to share it with. The murder of my one-time partner Glen Withers some time back, following not long after the death from cancer of Cyn, my ex-wife of many years earlier, had rocked me more than a little.

It wasn't that I thought myself a Jonah, or that I didn't feel a surge when an attractive woman came into view—like Lorraine Master—it was just that I sometimes wondered what the point was. In my experience sexual attractions, even love, were very transitory.

As I rinsed the dishes I remembered something I'd heard on the radio, maybe from Robin Williams on 'The Science Show', that in all creation only some kind of flatworm is truly monogamous and that's because it fuses with its partner first time up in coitus. Bad night ahead, Cliff, I thought. Go out and find some company.

I found it at the Toxteth, where else? Daphne Rowley, who runs a printing and photographic business in Glebe and has provided me with false IDs from time to time, was playing pool in the pub and gave a cheer when she saw me.

'A down-in-the-dumps PI named Cliff Hardy,' she whooped. 'I'm drinkin' for free tonight.'

She was right. We played for drinks and she won. I've beaten her on occasions, but only when I was up and being positive, as they say. Down and drinking, she whipped me. We ended up over brandies as the pub emptied. Daphne would be collecting her dogs from outside the pub.

'Tough case, Cliff?'

'Not so bad,' I said. 'I'm going off to New Caledonia in a couple of days.'

'Fuck you,' she said.

'Not original, Daph, I heard that earlier today. Just can't remember who from.'

The hangover was mild compared to some, but enough to need dealing with. I drove to the Redgum Gymnasium and

Fitness Centre in Leichhardt and did a moderately hard workout on the treadmill and the machines. Then into the sauna to sweat out the toxins. Feeling a bit light-headed but better, I came out to find Peter Lo doing curls with impossibly heavy free weights. Peter is Balinese and built low to the ground. I'd say that he's all bone and muscle except that would suggest he hasn't got a brain. In fact he has an excellent one. After climbing to a senior rank in the police force working in the forensic branch he's recently taken leave to do a doctorate in criminology. His thesis was something to do with justice and society.

'Hi, Dr Lo,' I said as he paused between curls.

He sighed and flexed his fingers inside his sweat-soaked mittens. 'If I had a dollar for everyone who's said that.'

'Sorry, Peter, I'm not at my best this morning.'

'Yeah, I saw you head for the sauna. Heavy night?'

'Not so bad. Can I buy you breakfast?'

'You mean, "I need your help", right?'

I nodded.

'Bar Napoli. Twenty minutes.' He sucked in air and his chest expanded like a balloon. He reached for a heavier weight. I couldn't bear to watch and went off to shower and dress.

Meeting Peter was no coincidence. Where I make it to the gym three times in a good week, he's there five mornings a week. They say that's too often but it'd be a brave man who'd tell Peter Lo that. I was sitting down with a black coffee and two plain croissants when he strode in. I signalled to Luigi, who brought Peter his standard order—black coffee and raisin toast, no butter.

'Let's dispense with the prelims, Cliff. The thesis is going okay, the wife and kids are fine, I bench-pressed a hundred and twenty-five kays this morning. Personal best.'

'I'm glad to hear it. How are your relations with your former colleagues?'

He took a bite of toast and appeared to chew it the prescribed number of times, whatever that is. He washed it down with some coffee. 'No problems.'

'Not afraid you're stealing a march on them, you being a slope and all?'

He laughed. 'Every one of them's just as competitive as me.'

'How about Karl Knopf?'

'What about him?'

'Your assessment.'

'Eat your breakfast. First class.'

I ate and drank. 'Would he talk to me if you asked him to?'

'What about?'

With Peter I was always upfront and honest. He was too intelligent and experienced to deal with in any other way. He saw through evasions and half truths immediately and responded appropriately. I told him about the Master trial and its peculiar tidiness.

'Karl's straight, he wouldn't be in anything dodgy.'

'Good. I'd just like to get his impression of the way things went down.'

'It *is* strange, the prosecutor shooting through like that. How about the customs guys?'

I shrugged. 'Dunno.'

'I'll ask Karl to give you a call and I'll see if I can find out anything about the customs men.'

'Thanks, Peter. I'll owe you. Again.'

He smiled. 'Never know, you could have given me a footnote.'

. . .

Worked out, saunaed, breakfasted and feeling pretty good, I phoned Lorraine Master at her office and Fiona put me through.

'Anything to report, Mr Hardy?'

'Not really. Nothing solid but I'm following up on a few things. I'm booked for tomorrow.'

'The money's there. I'm faxing you the PIN. Present ID at the bank and you'll be able to draw on the full amount.'

'You're sure I won't take off for Tahiti?'

'I'm sure.'

'What gym did Stewart go to?'

'Why?'

'Might be useful to ask around. See if anyone else has been asking around. See if anyone's interested that *I'm* asking around. It's a technique of the profession. It's called stirring the possum.'

'I see. Quaint. The Atlas, in Watsons Bay. I go there myself. You could ask about me.'

I let that go by. 'Why there?'

'It's a good gym. Plus it's close to the marina and the yacht club.'

'Stewart has a yacht?'

'No, Mr Hardy. I do, the *Merlot*, and Stewart doesn't know about it. It's that kind of a marriage. Is that all?'

More than enough, I thought. All I could say was, 'Thank you.'

The Atlas was located in a small street on the eastern edge of Watsons Bay. Unlike a lot of gyms—the Redgum, for instance, which has had earlier lives as a factory, a warehouse and dirty movie house—it didn't bear the signs of having once been something else. The cement block building with the landscaping and tiling and tinted glass couldn't have been more than a few years old and the discreet neon sign and name etched into the glass door were fresh and sparkling.

'Can I help you, sir?'

The young woman behind the desk was wearing a top that stopped just below her breasts and well above her track pants, revealing a perfect midriff. She was fined down and buffed up and jumping out of her skin to be helpful. Even after my workout and clean-out I suppose I still wore my look of an approaching use-by date. She arranged her sharp, low-body-fat features sympathetically.

'I'd just like to look around,' I said. 'Thinking of joining a gym, you know.'

'Sure. New to Sydney?'

Felt like an insult, but I took it. 'Up from Melbourne.'

The sympathy increased. 'Look, by all means, Mr . . .?'

'Master.'

'Mr Master. Everything's clearly signposted—weights room, machines, aerobics, sauna, pool.'

'Pool,' I said. 'That's nice.'

Her phone rang and she picked it up. 'Heated,' she said and her smile dismissed me.

It was mid-morning, and the place was busy. The free weights and machines sections were well patronised, mostly by yuppies but with a few oldies thrown in. Lines and wrinkles moving substantial weights, good to see. One sauna is much like another; the pool was a twenty-five metre job and would be very inviting at almost any time. I could see Lorraine Master here in her spandex with her personal trainer. What about Stewart?

At a gym there's always someone as interested in talking as working out, sometimes more interested. I spotted him in the weights room. He took every opportunity to chat to the other people there, worked the weights reluctantly and put them down gladly. A class started up on the aerobics floor and that took most of his attention. Well-toned women moving rhythmically will do that. I watched the whip-thin instructor bounce and strut and most of the class stay in sync. I felt my age and caught his eye as he towelled off unnecessarily. He wandered over.

'Gidday. Lookin' the joint over?'

'That's right. Not that aerobics stuff, though it's nice to look at.'

'Tried it once. Fuckin' near killed me.'

I gave him a conspiratorial nod. 'My brother comes here and I thought I'd take a look. Stewart Master, know him?'

He was a big bloke, fiftyish, balding, overweight but not too bad. Nothing he couldn't lose if he treadmilled, lifted more and talked less. 'Yeah, I know him. Knew him anyway. Bad luck, that.'

'Right, well I don't make a song and dance about it. I'm up from Melbourne to help his wife straighten things up a bit. It rocked the family. I mean, we knew Stewie was no angel, but drugs . . . not like him. Did you see much of him?'

He was cooling down and had to make a decision now whether to go on talking or go back to the weights. The talking won. He swigged from his water bottle and wrapped his towel around his shoulders.

'We chatted a bit, yeah. Not much. Nice enough bloke, Stewie. I'm Les, by the way.'

I played safe. 'Bob.' Forgettable.

We shook. 'Yeah, he mentioned he was from Melbourne. Talked about the AFL. Meant bugger-all to me. I'm a League man. Broncos. Ex-Queenslander. He put in serious time here. Going for tone rather than bulk, you know? But he was bloody strong. You'd be a fair bit older than him, eh?'

I grinned. 'I've lived hard. I'm not as old as I look. Still, I should've kept an eye on him.'

'Right, I know what you mean, but you can only do so much with a goer like Stewie. Still, it's going to be a blow to the people here.'

'How's that?'

'Stewie put in a bid to buy the place. Big, big bucks. Didn't you know? I thought . . . '

I clapped him on his beefy shoulder. 'It's all right, mate. Just playing it a bit close to the chest. Melbourne boy being cautious in the big smoke. Well, you never know. It could all work out okay. See you.'

Time to go. I didn't know whether I'd got away with it or not and wasn't going to hang around to answer questions. It was something to show for the visit. Hard to interpret. There'd been no reaction to the surname from the receptionist but it's not an uncommon name, and chances were she didn't know anything about the business side.

I walked away and looked back at the building. Freehold, very big bucks indeed, and even the price of the lease and the business goodwill would be heavy. I drove back to Darlinghurst and went to the office. Lorraine Master's fax with the PIN for an account with the Banque de France had come through. The card would be with me tomorrow, she said. I folded the sheet and put it in my wallet after writing the number in my notebook. Under the number I jotted two questions: did Stewart Master have that sort of money? Did Lorraine know about his interest in buying the gym?

I went out for a sandwich and when I got back there was a message from Peter Lo. I made instant coffee and rang him, talking between bites.

'Karl Knopf says he'll talk to you, Cliff. He's stationed in Darlinghurst so you could drop in and see him. Here's his number.'

'Thanks, Peter. He sounded interested, did he?'

'He did when I told him about the customs guys.'

I was about to take a bite but I dropped the sandwich on the desk. 'What?'

'Verdi was posted to Brisbane and Baxter to Perth.'

'Soon after the trial?'

'Right.'

'Something's going on.'

'Looks like it. Be careful, Cliff.'

'Why d'you say that?'

'Customs is federal. Don't get caught in the middle of a state and federal fuck-up. It's not a good place to be.'

I thanked him again and hung up. I finished the sandwich and the coffee without tasting them. Then I wet my finger and picked up the crumbs I'd dropped on the desk as I thought. In the old days I'd have smoked but now crumb-picking would have to do.

I dropped the sandwich wrapper in the bin and wandered to the window. St Peters Lane isn't much to look out on unless you happen to like the feel of old Sydney, which I do. It's narrow, trapped between the buildings that front onto William Street and the weathered sandstone of the church.

It's a sun-starved stretch, cold and windy in winter and shadowy in summer. There's no parking and it's never become a shooting gallery. It's not a place to linger in, so why was a man standing down there, staring up at my window and ducking out of sight when he saw me?

I'm mates with Stephanie Geller, aka Madame Stephanie, who runs a mail order, and these days online, astrological business in the office adjacent to mine. I have her key and occasionally let people into her waiting room when she's late.

'Zay like to be kept waiting, Cliff,' she once told me. 'So zay can feel zee vibes.'

She wasn't around, so I let myself into her office, which commanded a longer view of the lane than mine, and peeked out. No watcher. Had he followed me from Watsons Bay? Through all that traffic that's slowly strangling Sydney? No way to tell.

6

I PHONED Knopf but he wasn't interested in having me visit him at his place of business.

'I'd say it's time for a drink, wouldn't you?'

'Sure.'

'Know a place where there's never any cops?'

'Never? No.'

'I do.' He named a pub in Oxford Street with an almost exclusively gay clientele and said he'd be there in an hour.

'How will I know you?'

'I know you, Hardy. I was a shit-kicking constable when you used to hang around with Frank Parker. I was his driver for a while.'

'Sorry, I don't remember you.'

'Why would you? One hour.'

I put the phone down and tried to remember when Frank had a driver. He'd risen to Deputy Commissioner and had certainly had a driver then, but before that, as a chief inspector and a super? There must have been a few of them and they all blurred into one. Knopf sounded resentful and almost hostile, and nominating a gay bar? Looked like I was in for an interesting interview.

Years on the job should equip you to know if you're being watched or followed and to some extent that's true, but if the watcher or follower is good enough, and has enough cut-outs, it can be tough. I walked to where I'd parked the car, as alert as I could be for the false moves, the little slips, but there was nothing apparent. I started the engine and let the old Falcon warm up after sitting for a while on a cool day and busied myself with the choke while I looked around. I drove to within a couple of blocks of the hotel by a route that should have been tricky to track. Still nothing. Either not there or very, very good.

Friday night, early, but the buzz was starting to build. The difference in behaviour between gays and straights I reckon is not that much. Quiet straights and quiet gays go out early, drink and eat and go home. Party types go out late and drink, eat or don't eat, and stay out. The Beaumont Bar in the Prince Regent Hotel was dark and sedate, with k d lang playing softly in the background and a few pokies whirring quietly.

A couple of dozen people were scattered around, some at tables, some at the bar, some playing the pokies. Men and women, couples and singles, one group of three. All quiet. The barman, a handsome Polynesian wearing makeup and a pearl necklace, was the only person advertising. I ordered a beer and took a stool at the bar. The barman served it with a small bowl of nuts.

'You sure you're in the right place, brother?'

I lifted my glass. 'Sydney, Australia. You bet.'

He laughed. 'You're right there.'

A very tall, very slim man had walked in. Suede jacket, black T-shirt, earring. He nodded to a couple of people and to the barman. He shot out a hand that was thin and hard with rings on three fingers. 'Karl Knopf.'

I nodded. 'Cliff Hardy. I remember you now. You drove for Frank when he was a super. Too tall for the job, really.'

'That's right. He was a good bloke, Parker.'

'The best. What're you drinking?'

'What d'you expect, crème de menthe?'

'Let's get this straight—no, bad choice of words. You're gay and I couldn't care less. Okay?'

He smiled. 'Just having fun in a grey old world on a grey old day. Glass of red, Timmy, please. Bottle, not cask. Mr Hardy will pay. He's on expenses from a rich client.'

The barman uncorked a bottle and poured. 'Why can't I meet someone like that?'

'You mean Mr Hardy?'

'Shit, no, I mean his client.'

Knopf tilted his head to the left and we went across to a table at a distance from the other patrons. I took the nuts with me. We sat and we both had a drink and ate some nuts.

'So,' Knopf said. 'What d'you want to know?'

'Your impressions about the evidence presented in the Stewart Master case.'

'Four kilos of top grade heroin.'

'Handled by?'

'Master and Master alone.'

'Was that unusual?'

'No. The supplier usually wipes it clean.'

'Why didn't Master wipe it?'

Knopf shrugged. 'Didn't expect to be caught.'

'Careless.'

'Very.'

'I feel we're fencing, Senior. Did anything strike you as unusual about the evidence?'

'Like?'

'Christ, I don't know. Is it possible for someone's finger-prints to get on that sort of packaging without them ever having touched it?'

'You should've been his lawyer. It's possible. Prints can be transferred with the right technology. Highly unlikely though.'

'You weren't asked that?'

'No.'

'And you didn't volunteer it?'

'I was a witness for the prosecution.'

'Looking back?'

He shrugged and drank some wine. I'd finished my beer and a few of the salty nuts and was ready for a refill.

'Senior?'

'Don't call me that. It's Karl. It's impossible to say. It didn't come up at the time and I'd have to look at the stuff all over again from that perspective. And that's impossible.'

'Why?'

'Why d'you think? The stuff's been destroyed.' He finished his wine and got smoothly to his feet. 'My buy. Old, is it?'

I nodded. The place was filling up and the noise level was rising. Something louder was playing on the sound system and the pokies were buzzing along with the conversations. In days gone by the atmosphere would have been smoky. Not now. Knopf came back with the drinks and slid into his seat.

'Thanks,' I said. 'Peter Lo said you were interested when he told you the customs officers had been posted north and west. Why's that?'

He had white wine this time and took a long swig. His eyes moved around the room as if he was checking it out for the last time. 'Jesus, I don't know why I'm talking to you.'

'Yes you do.'

'You're right. Not long after the Master trial an offer came through for me to go on a study course.'

'Where?'

'Los Angeles. For a year, maybe two. Guaranteed promotion following.'

I took a long pull on the beer. 'Nice, but you refused. Why?'

'My partner's dying of AIDS. The anti-viral cocktail didn't work with him. Weeks to go. Their timing was a bit off.'

'I'm sorry.'

'Are you? He'll be glad to hear that.'

'Look, Knopf—'

'I know. I know. Chip on shoulder. Fuck it, it's all so unfair.'

We sat quietly for a while and sipped our drinks. He drew in a deep breath and pushed his empty glass aside. 'That's it for me. You?'

'I'm driving. Getting back to it, were there any unusual things about the evidence, the dope?'

'Yes. You're asking the right questions. The unusual thing was where it came from. Usually, you can trace the source pretty closely. It's a matter of the chemistry—the Middle East, India, Afghanistan, South-East Asia—they all have their own stamp. But this stuff was different. It was high grade all right, but different, and the worry was that it might be from another source.'

'Like?'

He shrugged. 'The Pacific someplace.'

'I see.'

'That was the worry. They didn't like the idea of a new close-to-home source opening up.'

'They?'

'*Los Federales.*'

'They were in it?'

'Up to their balls—leaning on me for the analysis, sending me samples and literature. I reckon that's why Master copped such a heavy sentence. I was told he was offered all kinds of leniency if he'd name names and talk places, but he never said a word.'

'You sound as if you admire him.'

'I was only in court a couple of days, but you had to kind of admire him. I mean, he's good-looking, great body, so . . . but apart from that. He had a kind of dignity.'

'Yeah, I saw him out at Avonlea the other day. He's still got it, I'd say.'

'What's he doing out there?'

I shrugged. 'Why not?'

'Like everything else, it's just a bit strange. Look, Hardy, I have to go. Hope I've been some help.'

We shook hands, both standing up. 'You have. Thanks. Just one thing. Why've you been so . . . open?'

He smiled and gave the first camp gesture I'd seen, a flick of the wrist as he consulted his watch. 'My partner's a cop as well. How do think they've treated him medically and professionally? I don't give a shit!'

When I was younger the sort of interview I had with Knopf would have left me empty and depressed, and even now I found it sobering. But the world's full of stories like that and it does no good to cry over them. Knopf struck me as basically tough. He'd recover from his loss and just maybe I'd learn something from this case that'd interest him. For now,

I had something to report to Lorraine Master before I started going through large amounts of her money. Always best to appear busy before clocking up the big ticket items.

It was raining steadily when I left the Prince Regent and I got soaked walking to the car. It was welcome after the dry spell but probably not enough to break it. Still, I kept my eyes open for any interested parties. No sign. Rain's never mattered to Sydney's Friday nightlife and the roads and streets were busy. Normally, I like that kind of bustle, but maybe Knopf's misfortunes were working on me because I was disinclined to go back to an empty house. I hadn't had a companion there for some time and there was no one on the horizon. I headed for the office where I could construct an encouraging email for my client with a few questions thrown in. At the office you don't expect cheery company.

The building was empty the way it mostly is after six o'clock and I turned on the stairwell lights' timer switches as I went up the two flights. I took off my wet jacket, dried my hair and face on a hand towel, made the obligatory cup of instant, settled down at the computer and tapped out my message with two fingers for the keys and my right thumb for the space bar. Works for me. I filled her in on the anomalies of the trial, told her when I was off to Noumea and that I'd received the authority for the money.

I sent the message and hit the 'Get message' button, not expecting anything. But there was a message: *You are interfering in matters best left alone. Be advised.*

My first threatening email. I printed it out and stored it. I imagined there were ways of tracking it to its source but I had no idea what they were and a strong suspicion that nothing would be learned anyway. I turned off the computer and the lights and left the office. Rain was spitting on the roof or I might have heard something. I didn't. The timer switch didn't work. They sometimes don't. In the dark I tripped on an obstacle placed at the top of the stairs and fell the full length of the flight.

I know how to fall, the army taught me—protect your head, roll when you hit. It works more or less, but not as well on stairs as on grass. I tumbled a bit and my head bounced off the wall once. I managed not to grab at things, which can dislocate a shoulder or an elbow. I hit the landing on my back and felt the wind rush out. The fall had loosened the dust and I coughed and spluttered but didn't black out so I heard the voice from below.

'Get the message, Hardy?'

7

THERE was no reply to my email when I limped into the spare room to check the computer. Limped because as well as a bump on the head and a bruised back I'd slightly twisted my ankle coming down the stairs the night before. Nothing a big scotch and three paracetamols hadn't coped with, but not the very best preparation for an international flight.

The questions that had sat in my sore head the night before were still there—who and why? And I still had no answers. It was hard to judge how serious the threat had been. A fall downstairs isn't so much, compared to the bashing I could've got in that dark space. But then again, I might've broken my neck.

I showered and soaked the ankle first in hot water and then in cold and rubbed it with goanna oil until the bathroom smelt like a changing room after a hard League game on a warm afternoon. They say rubbing does nothing useful except perhaps stimulate a bit of blood flow, but it felt better and I could walk without the limp. At least for now.

The brief rain had gone and the morning was clear. I'm not usually worried about flying, but I prefer the sky to be blue so the pilot can see where he or she is going. I tested the ankle by walking up to the travel agency to collect my tickets. No problems.

'Your flight's at 12.30 this afternoon, Mr Hardy,' the young woman who'd handled the matter said. 'Are you sure you've got everything in order?'

'Yep.'

'Have you hurt yourself? I thought I saw you limping.'

Back home, I packed. Tricky when you're not sure how long you're going to be away, but I travel light anyway and I figured that in New Caledonia underpants and shirts would dry overnight. I couldn't travel in my usual style because if I was meeting the white shoe brigade, which was what some of Stewie's mates sounded like, I'd have to tog up a bit. On a visit to Brisbane with a woman I'd spent some time with until she decided her time could be better spent, I'd bought a linen suit. It was 'unstructured,' which meant it didn't have shoulder pads and had a minimum of lining. Smart until it crumpled and still smart for a while after that. With old but classy Italian loafers and a black silk shirt, I reckoned I'd pass as someone who knew how to dress but only cared about it so far.

I hadn't opened the guide to New Caledonia or the French phrase book. I packed them into the overnight bag I use for travelling however long I'm away and put the sections of the Saturday papers I'd want to read into the snazzy carry-on bag the airline had provided along with a volume of Somerset Maugham's short stories. I was pretty sure there were some about New Caledonia. My only approach to a weapon, a Swiss army knife, went into the overnight bag.

Viv Garner, my long-suffering lawyer, had lost his wife six months earlier to a runaway cancer. They'd been very close and had no children so Viv was taking it hard, although he kept working and was as effective as ever. Saturday mornings, when he and Ros had done the shopping and played tennis, were bound to be desolate and he picked up the phone quickly when I rang.

'It's Cliff Hardy, Viv.'

'Cliff, good to hear from you. What's up?' The note of cheerfulness in his voice was forced, but maybe in time it would become natural again.

'Well, I want to pump you for information of course, but I thought I'd do you a favour and let you drive me out to the airport this arvo. I'm off to New Caledonia. Occurred to me you might like to share in the glamour and excitement, vicariously, like.'

He laughed. 'You bastard. Okay, you'll shout the drinks.'

'My client will gladly pay. How's an hour from now for you?'

I checked in and was told the plane would be leaving on time. Viv and I went to the bar and I ordered two double scotches. We hadn't spoken much on the drive, mainly about Ros and how Viv was coping. He seemed to be stronger than the last time and a lot better than the time before that. He told a few stories about times they'd spent together and his smiles were genuine.

He added a measure of water to his scotch and we clinked glasses. 'Okay,' Viv said. 'You've got about half an hour before you wing off to paradise. What gives?'

I filled him in, trying to give him a sense of the ways things had worked out at Master's trial. Viv is a solicitor but he's spent a good bit of time in the courts and he asked a few questions I could have answered better if I'd had the transcript, but he got my drift.

'Sounds funny,' he said. 'But trials are funny things anyway. What did you want to ask me?'

'What do you know about John L'Estrange?'

Viv drank some scotch and fiddled with a coaster. I noticed that his hands were shaking slightly and I wondered if he was on some medication. Maybe bringing him out here and putting scotch into him wasn't a good idea. 'John L'Estrange,' he said. 'Universally known as Jack the Odd. Successful barrister. Not in the top flight, as they say, but doing well. Said to have very strong political ambitions.'

'Jesus, that's all I need—state and federal police and politics thrown in.'

'You live in interesting times. But then, you always did, Cliff.'

'Yeah. Which party?'

'Oh, I think that would all depend.'

'Any rumours? Boys, girls, gerbils?'

'I'm a bit out of touch, but I don't think so. Just the politics.' Viv ran his hand over his bald head. 'He's got the looks—the figure, the hair and all that.'

That was enough for me to think about. We had another drink and chatted about nothing much until it was time for me to go. He gripped my hand and shook it solidly. No tremors. 'I'm glad you did this, mate. I love planes. I'm going to sit and watch them land and take off for a while.'

I browsed through the tourist guide as the Air Calin jet spent the usual waiting time on the tarmac and then seemed to taxi interminably to its take-off point. Courtesy of my client,

I was in business class with leg room. Economy, where I sit when I'm paying myself, looked to have the usual cattle-truck crowding. I spared them some pity as I leafed through the guide.

It seemed ridiculous for the islands to be named after Scotland by Captain Cook, but I suppose if we colonise Mars we'll do much the same. The French got hold of the place in the middle of the nineteenth century and have never really let go. A useful dumping ground for convicts, like Australia, it seems to have later become a source of timber and minerals for the home country, like Australia, and has ended up a tourist destination, like Australia. Without making the comparison, the guide told me that the Melanesians, the Kanaks, like the Aborigines, have battled for their rights against the French and made some headway.

I couldn't be bothered following the politics. There were accords and votes and plebiscites, which means money was spent and lies were told. It sounded like a tricky place to find your feet in but full of possibilities when you did. The same names kept cropping up and there was talk of 'development'. You could sniff yacht deals, silent business partnerships and no-questions-asked investment opportunities. I turned over the leaflets and maps the airline provided without great interest. A restaurant named Le Gaugin sounded intriguing but I was pretty sure I could bypass Palm Beach Curios.

The flight took nearly three hours and they served a good lunch with as much free wine as you could drink. French, too. I gave it a judicious sampling. Read the papers and a couple of the Maugham stories. The weather in Noumea, mild when I checked it in the paper a day or so before, had become hot and sticky in the interim. I had only one bag and nothing to declare other than the scotch I bought at the duty free, and I was through the bureaucracy pretty quickly. No language problems so far, although 'passport?' is much the same anywhere.

The Kanak woman at the car rental desk spoke good English and if she had doubts about my battered, non-gold American Express card she didn't let them show. Before very long I was in an air-conditioned Peugeot 307 with my jacket off and my T-shirt was starting to detach itself from my back. The rental had set Lorrie Master back quite a few thousand Pacific francs but I wasn't worried. For the moment, I concentrated on re-learning to drive on the wrong side of the road. I'd done it before in Europe and the US but not for some time and it's a freaky feeling reserved for Brits and colonials, as if the world has suddenly turned itself inside out. Noumea was fifty kilometres away, with other drivers to contend with, hills to climb, roundabouts to negotiate and crossings to survive. I reckoned that I'd have it programmed in by the time I arrived.

The drive wasn't bad once I'd relaxed into the road rules. The flat country gave way to hills which looked green in the distance and dry up close. Trees are trees to me, but most of these had a familiar look. I could've been in Australia except that every second car was a Renault, and those that weren't were Citroens, Peugeots and Fiats. A toll gate extracted some of the change I'd got by tending miserable Aussie dollars for the scotch, and when you start parting with money you know you're on the way to the big smoke. At a guess, an ugly structure in the near distance was the nickel smelter. The guide book had told me that the island was solid iron with lots of nickel. Good for them.

The city streets, with their roundabouts and intersections, were a test, particularly as I didn't really know where I was going, although the woman at the rental desk had tried to explain things to me. Not to worry. My plan in new places is to give myself plenty of time and basically get lost and get found and get lost again and so on. Eventually you get a sense of what's where. I knew that the hotel was at Ansa Vata and that was beachside. I found it by following half-understood road signs and by sniffing the air. Australians are mostly coast dwellers and have a feel for it. A few tourists with towels in hand helped to point the way.

The hotel was a big sprawling affair just across the road from the beach. The people at the desk spoke enough English for us to get by. No porters, which I like. Palm trees galore as you'd expect, good pool, 'fitness gym', and my room had a glimpse of the water. It was air-conditioned and perfectly okay. No mini-bar, which isn't always a bad thing, temptation-wise. Besides, I had the duty free scotch. I unpacked my few belongings, had a quick instant coffee with 'creamer', made a mental note to buy some milk, and headed straight for the pool.

After the swim and a short lie in the sun, I went back to the room, cracked the scotch and inspected my list of the names and locations Master had mentioned in his letters. Rory McCloud and Gabriel Rosito lived at something called the Costa del Sol and Reg Penny and Jarrod Montefiore at the Île de France, apartment complexes of some sort. Penny had a yacht, the *You Beaut*, moored at one of the two marinas. The Mocambo, the Ibis and the Park Royal hotel bars were favourite drinking places along with Le Saint Hubert brasserie and something called the Bout du Monde, which even my rudimentary French was up to—the End of the World. Master had also mentioned a place called Le Salon de Fun where there was lap dancing and a striptease. Master had stayed for ten days at the Meridien hotel where my guide put the tariff at the equivalent of four hundred bucks a day minimum, without breakfast. He'd rented a Saab and taken a plane trip to the Isle of Pines, paying for McCloud and Montefiore as well as himself. Stewie had been making a splash and wanted to tell Lorraine all about it.

I inspected my map and located the two residential tower blocks that housed Rosito and McCloud and Penny and Montefiore. The Île de France was hard up against the Hippodrome Henri Milliard, a racetrack, which sounded about right for a couple of Aussie punters, if that's what they were. The only Noumea local Master had named was Pascal Rivages, who sounded like the front man for the property deal the Australians were trying to put together. No detail on that.

There was nothing subtle about my plan. I intended to find all four men or as many of them as were still around and talk to them, singly or together, to see if they had any ideas about how Master came to be carrying the heroin. Then it was a matter of playing it by ear and if any cracks opened, trying to prise them wider with what is usually a good lever—money.

I'd worn a T-shirt under the suit on the plane and I put on a silk shirt now. It and the suit were a bit crumpled but I thought I still had the right look. I chose the Costa del Sol to try first because the guide said the Baie des Citrons which it overlooked was the place to go on a Saturday night. Maybe I could catch Gabriel or Rory before they hit the town and they could take me along. Lunch was a memory and the small scotch had put an edge on my appetite. I'd packed shorts and sneakers and promised myself a visit to the 'fitness gym' tomorrow.

It was well after 7 pm local time, an hour ahead of Sydney time, and the Baie des Citrons was starting to attract its customers. I walked the half kilometre to the tower as I could and forced myself to look left first and then right crossing the road. The place was solid cafés and brasseries for over a hundred metres and there were small boutiques and other shops tucked away here and there. The beautiful people were starting to congregate. The white ones, that is. The only black people I saw were serving the food and drink and most of them were on the beautiful side as well. I saw good examples of something you see all over the world—overweight, homely men accompanied by slender elegant women. Unusually for me, I was overdressed in my suit—light shirts, slacks and sandals were the order of the day.

Security at the Costa del Sol amounted to buzzing the tenant from the entrance lobby. Now that I thought about it, I hadn't seen any bars on windows, or security grills. It looked as if Noumea was a law-abiding town. Suited me. I was about to go in when I got the feeling that someone was watching me. I looked around but couldn't spot anyone. Paranoia goes with the job. I buzzed for McCloud and got no answer. Try Rosito.

'Yeah? Oui?'

'Mr Rosito, my name's Hardy. I'm a private detective from Sydney. Stewart Master's wife has hired me to look into things regarding her husband's drug conviction. Could I have a word with you?'

'Sure. Come on up and I'll give you a beer. It's good to hear an Aussie voice. Tenth floor, mate.'

As easy as that. I got in the lift and it went express to the tenth. The entrance had been neat and well appointed and the lift was functional without being flash. I wondered what it cost to stay at the Costa. To judge by the hotel tariff, where Lorrie was paying just under three hundred bucks a night, it wouldn't be cheap. One thing was for sure, the higher up, the dearer it'd be, and Gabriel Rosito was near the top.

He was standing at the open door with a Crown Lager in his hand. One-eighty centimetres maybe, 90 kilos—mostly muscle—shown off to good advantage in a tight white T-shirt and baggy shorts. Dark hair, deep tan. A heavy duty watch suggesting water sports or something involving impact. He looked to be about thirty and somehow I'd imagined Master's mates would be older.

He shot out a hard hand and we shook. 'Gidday. Have a beer. The local piss is okay but I thought you might prefer the genuine article.'

'Thanks.'

'Come in, mate. Make yourself comfortable.'

He had an easy way with him, not forced, as if he expected good things of everyone. A lucky guy from the lucky country. The apartment was large and light, tastefully furnished as far as my own limited grasp of taste could tell, with a magnificent view from the massive south-west facing window. I walked automatically towards it and heard Rosito's snort of amusement.

'Everyone does that. You can see clear to the islands from here on a good day. Bit cloudy now. You want a glass?'

I turned to see that he'd picked up his own bottle and was raising it to his mouth.

'No,' I said. 'Cheers.'

We both drank and looked at each other. 'I understand Stewie's wife's a looker,' he said.

'You could say that.'

'Blonde or what? He seemed to like blondes over here.'

'I forget.'

'Don't get your balls in a twist, mate. Just shooting the breeze.'

I wanted to get this back on the right footing. I took a swig of the beer and swilled it around. 'He's in Avonlea prison,' I said. 'None of this, no blondes, no brunettes.'

'Poor Stewie,' he said. 'What a mug to try something like that.'

8

GABRIEL Rosito and I got on well over the next hour with the aid of a few more Crown Lagers. The apartment was air-conditioned to a good level and as the light outside died the view glowed and then diminished quickly in tropical fashion as I'd seen it do in other places before—none of them as comfortable as this. Unless he was a superb actor, Rosito told me the truth from go to whoa. He and the other three had come to Noumea to try to acquire land to build a golf course resort closer to the city than those already in operation. Land was available on a 99 year lease but no foreigner could get the action without a local front man. My guess was right—Pascal Rivages was the guy and Stewart Master knew him from some earlier operation.

'Look,' Rosito said. 'We all knew that Stewie was a con artist and that Rivages was a crook. Useful bloke, but very suss. But it takes one to screw one, right? Reg, Jarrod and me all made money at home on the stock market, among other things, and—'

'What about McCloud?' I said, so as not to let the whole thing get too cosy.

Rosito shrugged. 'Dunno. Anyway, he's pissed off.'

'His name's still down there.'

'Quit detecting. So're names that've been gone longer. The joint's not exactly full. As I was saying, we had money to invest and needed tax breaks. We've all got managers and accountants yelling at us, you know? At least I have. Anyway, the idea came up and we decided to take a punt. I won't kid you, Cliff. Can I call you Cliff?'

I lifted my third beer in assent.

'Right. For one reason or another it suited us to come across here. I won't speak for the others, but I had a woman laying a paternity number on me. Bullshit, but you know how things can get. So we lobbed in and the thing got going. But it never really looked good. Too much politics. Too much bloody French bureaucratic bullshit and everything up for grabs after some local elections. Pascal had fingers in other pies and wasn't giving the plan the attention it needed. The Kanaks raised objections and some of the Caldoche had environmental concerns, or so they said.'

'Caldoche?'

'French New Caledonians, born here and identify with the place. Anyway, it all went pear-shaped and we cut our losses. Rory shot through after doing a bit of a tour around, sniffing at other things and Stewie . . . Another beer?'

I refused. I hadn't finished the third and didn't plan to. Although the flight hadn't been long and everything had gone smoothly, there's something unsettling about travelling those distances in that time. We aren't programmed for it yet and I was feeling weary. The beer was getting to me. Plus Rosito was smoking cigarillos and the room was fugging up. Also, I was feeling a certain level of disappointment. I had a sense that Rosito was exactly what he claimed to be and that he was telling the truth. There were just two more questions.

'Thanks for being so straightfoward,' I said.

He spread his hands. 'Nothing to hide, mate. After Stewie was arrested the cops here grilled us all. Not too rough, mind, but they had warrants and searched. Went through this place with a finetooth comb.'

'Ah . . . sorry, but why're you still here? It must be costing you a mint.'

He took a long draw on the cigarillo and expelled the smoke luxuriously. He was a man who enjoyed smoking as much as he enjoyed everything. 'No secret there either. You married, Cliff?'

'No. Divorced.'

He laughed. 'So am I, a couple of times. Have you noticed the women in this town? Sure you have. There's this Caldoche widow I've been seeing. Beautiful woman and very rich. Get it?'

I nodded and levered myself up out of the leather club chair. 'Last thing—are Penny and Montefiore still around?'

'As far as I know. Reg's running low on cash and trying to sell his yacht. You're more likely to find him at the marina than anywhere else. Jarrod talks pretty good French and he's got in with some people here. Passes himself off as *zoreille*— European French. Useful, that, because Pascal doesn't speak English. He helped me get on terms with the widow, but I haven't seen him for a while, come to think of it.'

I thanked him and he saw me to the door, saying we'd have a beer downtown sometime.

'Okay,' I said.

'You'd be on expenses, right? So we'll have a few.'

I left the Costa del Sol and set out to walk for a while to clear my head. The beer had dulled my appetite but the smells from the eateries would get to me eventually. Rosito had been helpful and the absence of McCloud had cut down on the work. A small speck of information would be worth noting—Lorraine Master had said that none of her husband's mates spoke French, but evidently Jarrod Montefiore did. Was that important? Too soon to tell.

I walked for a couple of kilometres around to the next bright lights spot, the Baie des Pêcheurs, and then back again. A brasserie not far from Gabriel Rosito's tower advertised itself as 'Friendly to Aussies and Kiwis'. I'm not proud. I took a seat and had a very good fish dinner with a small carafe of wine for not much more than you'd pay in Glebe Point Road. Better wine too, and great coffee. The waitress was tall, slim and beautiful in that cool French way, and her English was good so that I didn't have to stumble through the menu. The other diners were mostly tourists, Brits and others, with some locals thrown in.

I sat over the coffee longer than I would normally as the crowd thinned a bit, so that I'd have a better chance of spotting anyone taking an interest in me. I didn't. There were two ways back to the hotel—around the point on a well-lit footpath with the bay on the right, or across a stretch of rough ground that looked like a car park undergoing reconstruction. Less light. I had the Swiss army knife with me and I opened the small blade and kept my hand on it in my trouser pocket as I crossed the shadowy space. My mind was inventing scenarios the way it does: whoever attacked me in Sydney would send someone to have a go here—Rosito was Master's enemy and would put someone on my track—the whole Master thing was a fake and I was being set up as a pawn in some bigger game. Such things had happened before and probably would again. Not just now. I reached the street lights on the other side untouched by anything except the salty evening breeze.

People were taking the air along the beachfront and there were even a few in swimming. The local people sat in groups on the grass looking contented. Most of the women wore a long dress that looked to be inspired by the missionary-style Mother Hubbard, but they'd jazzed them up with bright colours and different trimmings. They looked good and if I'd had a woman at home I'd have brought her back one, but there was no candidate.

When I was younger I would've set out for the other tower or the marina or had a look-in at the nightspots Master had mentioned in his letters. My ex-wife Cyn had complained about my late hours or, rather, my early hours, which was usually the time I arrived home when I was working on a case. I could still do it when I had to, but after an international flight and the amount of work I'd done, as well as a certain lack of urgency associated with the job, I was ready to call it a day. It wasn't as if Master was scheduled for execution. In fact, when I thought about it as I climbed the stairs at the hotel, he really hadn't seemed all that unhappy to be where he was. Or maybe I wasn't reading him right. He was a con artist, after all.

The hotel contained several restaurants and bars and there was some activity in all of them and some late night frolickers in the swimming pool. I was tired and my mind was drifting. Cyn and I hadn't had a honeymoon. Both too busy. I'd gone to holiday places with other women. To Bali with Helen Broadway. To Port Douglas with . . . who? Cyn might've liked this place. She could've exercised her school-girl French. But Cyn was dead and I was working. I worked the key in the awkward lock and opened the door. A welcome waft of cooled air hit me first, and then the realisation that my room had been thoroughly searched by someone who didn't care that I knew.

Who can get into a locked hotel room? Anyone who really tries. There are lots of ways and I've used some of them myself. Had I told Rosito where I was staying? I thought I had. Did I have to revise my assessment of him? I didn't think so. At least I was able to acquit myself of paranoia. Someone in Noumea was interested in me and was taking steps. I wished them luck. There hadn't been a single thing in the room that would have told them anything. I had my notebook, the photocopies of Stewart Master's letters and everything to do with Lorraine Master's money box in my possession.

It got light early but I had the curtains drawn, the air conditioning on low and I slept well. The hotel must have had a lot of early risers because there seemed to be a lot of used places at breakfast. Maybe they were at church. I opted for the continental and took the juice, fruit, croissant and coffee out to a table near the pool. As I'd been strolling home last night I'd thought I might pay an early morning call to the gym. Maybe later.

I was in shorts, T-shirt and sandals and fitted right in except for the lack of a good tan. Thanks to my Irish gypsy grandmother's genes, my skin never goes really pale and I'd brown up pretty quickly here. The day was already warm with a clear sky and those tropical smells that tell you you're a long way north of home. I was mulling over how best to proceed when I caught a whiff of cigarette smoke and was suddenly in the shade.

'Bonjour, Monsieur Hardy. May I join you?'

A tall, heavily built character with a Polynesian look to him was standing by the table and blocking the sun. He wore black trousers and a white shirt. Balding, forty-plus and with outsized hands the way they get from years of physical labour. The cigarette looked like a matchstick in his thick fingers. You have to watch yourself around hands like that. Not the kind of guy you say no to straight off.

I managed a muttered 'Bonjour', and motioned for him to sit down a split second before he did anyway.

'Are you enjoying your stay in Noumea?'

'I'm here on business, Monsieur . . .?'

He took a long drag on his smoke instead of answering. 'You must try the casino. I assume you got your vouchers when you arrived. Five hundred francs free to begin with, n'est ce pas?'

'I'm not a gambler. I don't want to be rude, but I'm trying to eat my breakfast.'

'Of course. I'm sorry. There's someone who would like to speak with you. The gentleman over there.'

I looked in the direction of his inclined head. A man wearing a suit something like the one hanging up in my room, except that it wasn't wrinkled and he wore it with a shirt and tie, was sitting at a nearby table. He wasn't looking at us.

'He'd like you to join him.'

'Who is he?'

'He will tell you.'

I tore the rest of my croissant in half and applied a dob of the butter that had pretty well melted while we were talking. I put it in my mouth, chewed and took a sip of the cooling coffee. 'He's welcome to join *me*. I'm happy here, except that you've made my coffee get cold.'

He got up smoothly and walked across to where the other man sat. I noticed that he butted his cigarette in an ashtray on a empty table before he got there. He stood and they had a brief conversation. The man in the suit smiled and waved the other guy away as he moved towards my table. The man who hadn't identified himself melted into the background, but I had the feeling that he'd never be very far away from whoever this was.

'Mr Hardy. I am Pascal Rivages. Welcome to Noumea.'

The voice was low and pleasant, heavily French-accented. He knew I'd know the name and that it would catch me on the hop just a bit, and he enjoyed his moment. Couldn't blame him. He was a well-preserved fiftyish with a fair skin he'd protected from the sun and a facial bone structure that would carry the years well. His dark hair was clipped close, like his moustache. Faint touch of grey.

'Bonjour,' I said.

He laughed. 'I'm sorry about sending Sione to you. That was a little heavy-handed.'

'He looks like a handy type.'

'I'm sorry. My English . . . handy . . .?'

'Useful.'

'Yes, very useful. I understand that your coffee is cold. Some more?'

'If it's no trouble.'

'It's no trouble, Mr Hardy. I have an interest in this hotel. A considerable interest. I also have an interest in the car hire firm you've used.'

He signalled to a waiter and I pushed my cup and plate aside. 'Mr Big?' I said.

The melodious laugh came again. 'Oh, I wouldn't say that. Not at all. Just un homme d'affaires. How's your French?'

'Not as good as your English. Are you threatening me?'

A Kanak waiter brought coffee, cream and sugar on a tray and Rivages watched his every movement closely. When the operation was over he nodded and favoured the waiter with a smile that would make his day. 'I don't threaten people, Mr Hardy. Not any more. I don't have to. Gabriel Rosito told me what your business is in Noumea. I can assure you that you are on . . . what do you call it? A wild goose chase.'

I poured myself some coffee from the silver pot and added a couple of cubes of sugar. 'I find the coffee here a little bitter,' I said. 'I've been on lots of wild goose chases. Sometimes you catch the goose.'

'Peut-être . . . perhaps. I wouldn't want you to waste your time.'

I sipped some coffee. Not bitter, never was. 'I'm being paid for it. And now I'm curious why an important man like yourself would bother to talk to me.'

'Ah, it's nothing to do with your business here. I made enquiries about you. You have criminal convictions and—'

'One.'

'—a reputation for causing trouble. Noumea is a quiet, law-abiding place, as you must have observed.'

I was getting tired of him with his smooth velvet glove manner. 'Yeah,' I said. 'It strikes me as being like a dull French provincial city on its best behaviour. Needs a bit of livening up.'

That reached him. A flush rose in his face and his hand twitched. For a moment I thought he might toss his coffee cup, still empty, at me. He fought for control and didn't like doing it. At a guess, he was a man who'd had it all his own way for a very long time and couldn't handle recalcitrance. He pushed his chair back and stood. I caught a movement behind me that was probably Sione and my skin crept a bit.

'Be careful,' Rivages said.

'Toujours,' I said. But I was saying it to his back.

I drank the rest of the coffee and thought it over. I had the answer to who searched my room. Gabriel Rosito must have got on the blower to him pretty quick smart, so he wasn't quite the what-you-see-is-what-you-get guy he came across as. Almost certainly he'd alerted the others so that I could expect a guarded reception from them, or perhaps no reception at all. Probably needed to move quickly. One stray point I'd picked up. Why had Rosito said Montefiore was useful in their dealings with Rivages because he could speak French? Rivages spoke all the English he needed to. But maybe Rosito didn't know that.

The day had warmed up quickly and the pool was inviting. A quick gym session followed by a dip would have been good, but I had things to scribble in my notebook and places to go and people to see, if they were still around.

9

Penny or Montefiore? The marina or the Île de France tower? I fancied the sea air and drove to the first of the two marinas. No boat called *You Beaut*, a name that seemed to mystify the French speakers I questioned, or maybe it was just my halting phrase-book French and bad accent. A lot of money bobbing along on the water here, and if you had enough of it yourself you could charter a luxury game fishing boat to go out and catch marlin. Pretend you were Zane Grey or Lee Marvin, Hemingway even. All as dead now as the fish they were so fond of catching.

Noumea came into its own a bit down here. The Gare Maritime des Îles had a genuine working port look to it with slightly rusty, battered cargo boats loading and unloading. Apparently there was a lot of trade and cargo shifting between the islands and these ships did most of it. Somerset Maugham territory, possibly still with alcoholic doctors and tormented captains.

The second marina was across the way—more money and frolicking in the sun. I located Penny's boat moored about halfway along it. I know nothing about boats. The *You Beaut* was white and big, sharp at one end and blunt at the other. It had a lot of brass railing and a high cabin mounted near the front with a long aerial waving in the light breeze. It looked very clean, almost too clean, and I remembered that Rosito had said Penny was trying to sell it. It had the same look as a house a day or two away from the auction when the owners run around picking up every scrap of paper and wiping away every spot of dirt.

I stood on the dock and hailed the boat in a tentatively loud voice. A number of other owners were working on their boats or lazing about. They took an interest in me and I was out of place as someone obviously non-nautical. 'Hello, the *You Beaut*,' I yelled, feeling silly doing it and even sillier when I had to do it again.

A man's head followed by his body appeared from the middle of the boat. He was tall and spare and looked as if he'd been born out in the sun and never gone inside. He was the colour of teak with sun-bleached hair and long, toned muscles in all the right places. All he wore was a pair of denim shorts faded to the colour of his eyes. He held a mobile phone in his hand and he gestured for me to wait while he spoke into it. A few words, that was all.

'Are you Hardy?'

'That's right.'

'Come aboard.'

I eased down onto the short gangplank; a section of the railing had been slid clear and I stepped through to the deck. Penny dropped the mobile into the back pocket of his shorts and stuck out his hand.

'Gidday. Reg Penny.'

'Cliff Hardy, but you know that.' I shook a hand with more calluses on it than smooth skin. 'Who told you? Rosito or Rivages?'

'Both, mate. I've been expecting you. Gabe said you liked a beer. Want one?'

'No, thanks. Bit early. So you know why I'm here.'

'Sure. All about Stewie Master. We'd better get out of the sun, you're gonna burn. Doesn't feel that hot but it's deceptive. Follow me and watch your head.'

Barefooted and agile, he moved forward, instinctively ducking under ropes and other nautical things I'm ignorant of. The boat was bobbing gently at its mooring. I was in deck pants, a sports shirt and sneakers and felt overdressed, again. I followed him to a hatch and down a set of steps to a tight space with a built-in bench, seats and kitchen fittings.

Both big men, we wedged ourselves in on either side of the bench. Penny gestured at the stove. 'I could make coffee or something.'

I shook my head. 'No, thanks. I suppose you're just going to confirm everything Rosito said to me—you don't know anything about Master and drugs. All news to you. Poor Stewie. Business deal fell through and you're just here trying to sell your boat.'

He surprised me then by throwing back his head and letting out a bellow of a laugh that ended in an alarming wheeze. 'That fuckin' Gabe. He's full of shit. Most of what he said's right but I'm not selling the yacht. Yacht, not boat. No way.'

'Why would he say that?'

He shrugged. 'Who knows? That's Gabe. Always sorta big-noting. Him and his Caldoche widow. You heard about that?'

I nodded.

'She's a looker all right, but he's got Buckley's.'

'What about Rivages?'

'What about him?'

'He fronted up to me at the hotel this morning, or rather his heavy did.'

'Sione.'

'Right. Sione.'

'Don't worry about it. It's all just fun and games. Pascal likes to come on as . . . you know.'

'The Abe Saffron of Noumea.'

He laughed again. 'Yeah, and it's about as real as that. There's no fair dinkum crime here. The lid's on the joint real tight. Everyone's got it too cushy.'

'So where did Stewart Master get a couple of keys of heroin?'

'Search me, mate. I've got no idea.'

I examined him closely before I spoke again. He was older than he looked, possibly in his mid-forties and keeping the years at bay with physical activity. The hair was receding a bit and on inspection the yacht wasn't quite as spiffy downstairs as up on top. The paperback books and magazines on a shelf had a well-thumbed look and there was a flat, almost empty, small packet of cigarette tobacco. Rollies, the economic choice.

I leaned slightly towards him across the bench top. 'I didn't mention this to Rosito, but I've got some money to pay out for information.'

'How much?'

'Depends. Why're you guys all so defensive and sticking together? Why did Rivages virtually threaten me? Why did Rory McCloud shoot through?'

He screwed up his face in order to think about it and crow's feet leapt into life around his eyes. His mouth and chin sagged a little, I noticed. He wasn't quite the boyo he made himself out to be. The old shorts fitted the image but the oil ingrained into the pads of his fingers and the dirt under the nails suggested that he was having trouble with his engine. Eventually he made up his mind.

'I'll be honest with you, Hardy. I'd like to get out of here but I'm strapped for cash. The engine's buggered and the rest of the equipment isn't too flash for a long sail.'

'Where would you go?'

'What d'you reckon? Back to Australia. Beats this place to a frazzle. I need nine or ten grand. Could you run to that?'

'Have to be good information.'

'It would be, but I'd have to have the money real quick so I could leave pronto.'

'What's quick?'

'Today. Tomorrow at the latest.'

'That's quick all right. Give me a taste.'

He stroked his beaky nose the way some people do when they're trying to decide. He looked around the cabin at the faded books and the torn curtain only half covering a port-hole. It occurred to me that he hadn't made up his mind about selling the boat and didn't want to. Maybe I was giving him an out. He stopped stroking and decided.

'Okay. One, Rory didn't shoot through of his own accord. He disappeared. Two, Jarrod Montefiore's the guy you need to see. He's got a story to tell and he'll tell it for the right kind of dough. I know where he is or at least I can find out. Gabe and Pascal don't.'

'He's not at the address I've got, the Île de France?'

'Moved out like me. Similar reason.'

I thought about it while he fidgeted, scratching at some sun spots on his hands. 'That's why you'd have to p.o.q. Because of Rosito and Pascal?'

He made a zipping motion across his mouth. It was a bit theatrical, but there was something in his faded eyes that spoke of concern, even fear.

'Okay,' I said. 'I'll go into town and get the money. I'll give you five straight off and the rest after I talk to Montefiore. That could be whenever you can arrange it.'

'Deal. I'll send someone with you to get the five.'

'How do I know five isn't enough to get you on your way?'

'You don't, but it isn't.'

'I have to tell you I've had a feeling that my movements are being watched. Does that worry you?'

'Yes,' he said. 'But I'll take the chance.'

I drove to the bank with a silent young Kanak whose name I never learned. On presentation of my passport, the card and keying in the PIN, I was told that I could draw on the sum of close to fourteen million Pacific francs. An image of Cagney on top of the electricity supply station flashed into my mind: *I made it, Ma. A millionaire!* My mother would've laughed and ordered a champagne cocktail instead of a Para port.

I gave the youngster the equivalent of five thousand Australian dollars and he walked away without a word as if he was a mute. Maybe he was. I was finding Noumea stranger and more interesting by the hour. I'd told Penny where I was staying and he said he'd send a message when he had the information.

I walked around until I found somewhere to have a drink and a think in that order. By chance it was the Saint Hubert, one of the places mentioned in Master's letters. I went to the bar and bought a Heineken. The glass had a plimsoll line on it so that you could tell you were getting the right amount of beer with the froth as extra. Not something I could see catching on at home. There was a bowl of nuts on the bar, a touch long departed from the places I usually drink at, and I took a modest handful over to a seat where I could look out at the city square and the passing parade. It also gave me a chance to spot interested parties.

The place had a lot going for it—a very good-looking barmaid, reasonable lighting, cooling fans and a good semi-outdoors feel. I could see why the Aussies would choose it as their watering hole. The fact that a standard beer cost the equivalent of seven Australian dollars would keep the riffraff away but would make a round pretty expensive. I hadn't seen any drunks about, perhaps because a good skinful would cost more than it was worth. I sipped the beer and studied everything around me, still and moving, and decided that if I was being watched, the watcher was so good I'd never spot him anyway.

I had a positive feeling about Penny. There was an edge of desperation about him that just might make his contribution valuable. But then again, I'd thought Rosito was a straight shooter and that had turned out to be wrong. I told myself you can't expect to read all the signals correctly in a foreign place. That was worth a few nuts and a good pull on the Heineken. But you can't afford to get them consistently wrong either. The bar overlooked the city square, which had a neat, sculptured French look like the town itself. It was something like Nice, something like Marseilles, places I'd visited briefly a long time ago. If the job panned out right maybe I could go again.

I finished the beer and drove to the Île de France to check the tenant list. No sign of Penny or Montefiore. Also no sign of my tail of the day before. Maybe Rivages thought that his warning would do the trick. Or maybe he just didn't care. I felt that I'd made reasonable progress for the time and money expended, and decided to take it easy until I heard from Penny. I went back to the hotel, swam and lunched and slept.

Later in the afternoon I did the tourist bit. I caught a ferry to the Île aux Canards, a coral atoll a kilometre or so offshore. No jetty, you waded a couple of metres to get on the boat. The crowd was thinning out from what had evidently been a busy day, but there were still people lying on thick blankets over the spiky coral and some swimming and snorkelling in the crystal water. I had a dip, had a drink at the bar and caught the ferry back. Pricey at every point, but innocent.

I had another swim in the pool and ate dinner at the Japanese restaurant in the hotel, encouraged by the fact that several groups of Japanese tourists were there already. Nothing adventurous—miso soup and teriyaki fish and a half bottle of the good dry French plonk. Signed for it, went back to my room, watched some cable news on TV and was in bed with the Maugham stories well before midnight. Nothing had been disturbed in the room and there were no messages for me. Not a bad day, I thought as I settled down. Thanks, Lorraine. Tough luck, Stewie.

10

I HAD an undisturbed breakfast and I hung around the room for a while hoping for a call. Then I had a swim and took a couple of looks at the message board at the reception desk. Nothing. The morning was wearing on and I was getting impatient, certainly not settling into holiday mode, something I've never been that good at anyway. 'Driven,' Cyn used to say, 'and it's driving me crazy.'

I showered and drank some more instant coffee with creamer. I was thinking of going to see Penny when a light tap came at the door. It was the non-speaking Kanak youth again. He handed me a piece of paper and slipped away before I could thank or tip him.

I unfolded the paper and examined the block-capitalled address and then pulled out my tourist map. Nothing wrong with playing the visitor. The address was in the heart of Noumea's Chinatown. Just to be sure I took the most indirect route I could so that anyone consistently behind me had to be following. Nobody. The address turned out to be a shabby-looking block of flats on a street corner above a cluster of trade stores selling, as far as I could tell, exactly the same things at exactly the same prices.

No security here—just a set of dilapidated steps going up from the street beside one of the stores. My information was that Montefiore was in flat five. Turned out to be on the top level where the smell of neglect was strongest and the light was the least good. It was hot and I was sweating when I found the door. The only light was from a landing window that hadn't been washed this century and a good bit of the last. Still cautious, I paused at the top of the stairs, looked and listened. Nothing. I stepped over a broken carton spilling beer cans and knocked at the door of flat five.

I heard a faint sound inside, possibly a radio or television, and then it stopped. I knocked again and got no response. If an Australian wheeler-dealer named Jarrod Montefiore, who hung out with types like Master, Penny and Rosito and spoke French, was staying in this dump there could only be one reason. He was hiding. Why not somewhere better? Not hard to guess. I pulled out the wad, detached a ten thousand franc note worth about a hundred and forty Australian dollars, and slipped it under the door. I put my mouth close to the jamb and spoke in a voice I hoped would carry only to where I wanted it to be heard.

'My name's Hardy. I'm a private detective from Sydney working for Stewart Master's wife. I've seen Rosito and Rivages and haven't got along with them all that well. Reg Penny gave me this address. Or rather, I bought it. I'm giving him ten grand to get clear of Noumea. I can do the same for you or maybe more depending on what you can tell me.'

When I'd finished I pushed another note under the door and stepped back. I heard bare feet on the floor and a slight groan, the kind you make bending down if you're old or injured. I bent and pushed another note through the gap.

Over four hundred bucks. Had to be reasonably serious money for a man living here.

'How do I know you're not lying?' The voice was strained and croaky—too much smoking or maybe some other cause.

'Ring Penny on his mobile. He'll tell you.'

'I haven't got a phone. How do I know—'

'Listen, mate, if I wanted to do you harm I'd have kicked in this shitty door by now and done it. Stewie Master's wife has given me a fair bit of money to spend finding things out. Penny's got some and he's getting some more. How about you? Want a plane fare to Sydney or Brisbane or bloody LA and some spending money, or d'you want to stay in this pisshole?'

I heard a sigh as the lock was released and the door swung open. The man who stood there was a wreck, but a recent wreck. He was close to 190 centimetres tall and the singlet and track pants gave evidence of an athletic build. His left arm was in a sling and he had a cast on the lower part of his right leg. There was a heavy slab of tape over his nose and his mouth was swollen and puffy with a dark scab along the lower lip. I've had some beatings in my time and delivered some, but this was a beauty.

'Jesus,' I said, and I suddenly had a flash of the sort of man who could do a job like this. 'Sione?'

He nodded and the effort hurt him. 'You do know a fuckin' thing or two, don't you? Come in.'

He hobbled aside. The cast had a metal heel on it so he could walk. Better than a crutch but not much better. I've tried both. The flat was as ramshackle, dirty and comfortless on the inside as the building itself looked from the street. We went straight into the living room-cum-kitchen and the area was a sea of beer cans, butt-brimming ashtrays and saucers and take-away food containers. The furniture was threadbare and flies buzzed around the kitchen area and made sorties out to where we stood.

Montefiore—it had to be him—leaned against a wall and then slid down into a fragile-looking Chinese saucer chair that held his weight, just. His mane of dark hair was slightly streaked with grey—could've been distinguished if it hadn't been greasy and matted. He smiled and I saw a gap where a couple of front teeth should have been. 'Pretty shitty, eh?'

I eased down into a plastic chair after flicking away an empty Winfield packet. I nodded. 'It'll do.'

He snorted. 'Haven't got any dope on you by any chance?' 'No.'

He shrugged. Despite the broken arm the musculature was intact, but it wouldn't be unless he got into some physiotherapy pretty soon. 'How's Reg doing?'

'On his uppers. Reckon he sold you out?'

'No, we're mates in this fuckin' mess. You must be the genuine article. How much money are we talking? Sorry I can't offer you anything.'

'Don't worry about it. The money part doesn't work like that. That'd be like telling the reserve price at an auction. Penny gave me a taste before I bought. You're going to have to do the same.'

'Give me a clue.'

'Rory McCloud.'

'Disappeared. Suspicious circumstances.'

'Okay,' I said. 'You're on "go".'

Montefiore excused himself and left the room. I heard water running and when he returned he'd made an attempt at combing his hair, had washed his face and had shrugged into a creased but clean blue sports shirt. He had beach scuffs on his feet and I could smell toothpaste over the competing smells in the flat, mostly dirt, take-away food and stale tobacco.

He sat where he'd sat before. 'Sorry I can't offer you a drink or anything.'

'Don't worry.'

'So you're paying Reg ten grand.'

'Nine or ten.'

'Must think all his birthdays have come at once. Just for putting you on to me. I reckon what I can tell you must be worth twenty, twenty-five.'

'Could be. I'll have to be the judge.'

He scratched at his stubble. 'Problem would be living to spend it and getting Fay out with me.'

'Fay?'

'Girlfriend. Fay Lewis. One of the Kiwi Kuties.' He found a leaflet among the mess beside his chair and passed it over to me. It advertised the Kiwi Kuties, performing nightly at the Salon de Fun—'lap's dancing and stripe tease' among the attractions. The leaflet showed three blondes in minuscule outfits top and bottom plus white Stetsons and high-heeled knee-high boots. Lots of stars and spangles, a suggestion of the American flag. Good war-against-terrorism stuff. The three women looked identical.

'Fay's the one on the end,' Montefiore said.

I shrugged. 'Left or right and how can you tell?'

'Fuck you,' he said. 'Anyway, she's more a part of this than you think. She's got a photograph you'd be very interested in.'

'You'd better get me interested, then,' I said. 'I don't want to spend any more time here than I have to. Might catch something.'

Montefiore wasn't a gifted storyteller. He backtracked, repeated himself and fumbled for the right expression. Also, he threw in some French words here and there and I had to ask for a translation. What he had to say boiled down to this: after the property deal fell through the five Australians decided to hang around Noumea for a while looking for other opportunities. McCloud, Penny and Montefiore were approached by a man with a proposition—help to set up Stewart Master as a drug smuggler taking a small amount of heroin into Australia and they'd be in for a big reward. Not only cash in hand, but the green light from the federal and state police to handle a big marijuana consignment going into Australia. The stuff was coming down from South-East Asia and Pascal Rivages was handling the Pacific trans-shipment.

McCloud's reaction was to threaten to go straight to the police and to tell Master, who was away elsewhere on the island. 'They'll fish him and his car out of deep water somewhere one of these days,' Montefiore said.

Penny said he wasn't interested one way or the other, which disappointed the man because he'd thought of Penny's yacht as the delivery vehicle. The idea was to land the water-proofed bales on a reef off the coast and then move it to the mainland. Penny was warned anonymously to keep his mouth shut and certain things began to go wrong with his boat. He was burgled and lost most of his available cash. Montefiore reckoned that Mr X and Rivages wanted him to stick right there in Noumea where they could keep an eye on him.

'I played along for a while to see if I could make a dollar out of it. I never had any intention of going through with it and when that became obvious, Rivages had Sione work me over. But good.'

'Rosito?'

Montefiore shook his head. 'Gabe's got plenty of money. More than the rest of us put together. All he's interested in is cunt. They knew they couldn't get to him.'

Montefiore said he didn't know how it was done but the plan went through. Master was nabbed and convicted. He presumed that Rivages got his shipment through and that everything was hunky-dory.

'Question one,' I said. 'Who was this mastermind?'

'I don't know his name.'

'Tell me everything about him you can think of.'

'Jeez, I wish I had a drink.'

'Later. You're doing well. You'll be able to afford a few.'

'Okay. Australian, mid-thirties, medium-sized, maybe a bit bigger. Not that fit. Ordinary looking, mousy hair, nothing unusual except . . . I'd swear blind he was a cop. He had the manner, you know? Sort of special in his own fuckin' head.'

I nodded. 'Scars, mannerisms, habits? Come on.'

Montefiore scraped at his stubble as if the rasping sound would trigger a memory. 'Didn't smoke. Drank mineral water in the pub. Jesus, yes, he had BO. He was scrubbed clean, shaved close, short back and sides, fresh shirt and daks, but he still had this whiff of BO.'

'Good. Question two. Why're you still around and in this dump?'

Montefiore had taken a bad beating and was down on his luck, but he wasn't a man without self-esteem. From the look on his face I could tell he'd have hit me if he'd been able and he wanted to tell me to go to hell because he couldn't. 'I ran out of money and this is the best I can do. At least Rivages doesn't know where I am.'

'Why does that matter?'

'I reckon he's still making up his mind what to do with Reg and me. He doesn't like us knowing what we know. He's got fingers in lots of pies—property, gambling, politics. We could damage him if we talked. Equally, if we went missing like Rory it wouldn't look good.'

'Can't he buy the cops?'

Montefiore shook his head and looked tired all of a sudden. 'No. Not here. He's obviously in with that Australian cop so I don't know if we'd even be safe back at home. If I get out of this I'll take off for somewhere else as quick as I can. New Zealand maybe, Fiji, Bali . . .'

'Okay. You've earned some money, but I've thought of something else. If Rosito's not in on it, why did he get in touch with Rivages so quickly?'

'Just playing safe. Silly fucker reckons Pascal can help him with the widow. Like I told you, he—'

'Yeah. What about you and this Kiwi? Let's get back to her, and you and her.'

'I'm crazy about her. She's amazing. She'll go with me if I've got money.'

I grinned. 'That doesn't sound like a match made in heaven.'

'Get stuffed. See this?' He grabbed at his hair. 'I'm not a kid any more. I've led a weird, rough life and I don't expect to make old bones. I want to grab what I can while I can.'

'Fair enough. So, this photograph?'

'She's got a Polaroid of the cop. Not good, but good enough.'

I sat quietly and thought it over. Montefiore went out of the room and he seemed to be moving more easily all of a sudden. Hope'll do that to you, I guess. But it could've been something else. He came back with two mugs.

'Instant coffee. No milk. Best I can do. What're you thinking about, Hardy?'

'One of the things I'm thinking is about how everyone I meet in this bloody thing seems to be lying to me. My client told me none of Master's associates spoke French. You do. Rosito told me Rivages didn't speak English; he does. He also told me Penny was trying to sell his boat. He says he won't. See what I mean?'

'About the languages, everyone does that here—pretends not to speak or understand. It can give you an edge. Hey, there's a guy on the local TV, speaks good English. He asked the station to pay for some language training. They wouldn't. So now he won't talk a word of English. Uses an interpreter on the program, costs the station dough, and everyone knows he understands just about every word that's said to him in English. See?'

I sipped some of the coffee. For black instant it wasn't bad. French Nescafé? 'What about you, Montefiore? You're lying about something. I know you are but I just can't put my finger on it.'

It was his turn to drink coffee and ponder. He shook the hair out of his eyes, put the mug down on the floor and let his arm slip out of the sling. He extended the arm and flexed his fingers. He thumped the heel of his cast on the floor a few times while keeping his eyes locked on mine.

'I'm coming good, Hardy. I was the light-heavy kick-boxing champion of Queensland. Two men held me while Sione went to work. I'm hoping to get a shot at him, man to man.'

11

I WASN'T interested in tackling Sione myself, but that was Montefiore's problem. I agreed to pay him fifteen thousand for his information as well as the photograph. If for some reason we couldn't get the photo, I'd scale it down to an unspecified level. Had to keep him on his toes because, although I now had a story to tell Lorraine Master, some physical evidence would make it a lot more convincing. I gave some thought to the possibility that this could be a set-up. The Kiwi woman could be holding a photograph of no one in particular who matched the description Montefiore had given me. Easy money. But it seemed unlikely that anyone could've anticipated me and my offer.

I went to the bank to draw more money and bought a few things for Montefiore on the way back—a shirt, shampoo, deodorant, shaving tackle and such; a six pack of the local beer, milk, fruit, bread and cheese. When I returned he'd made an effort to clean up the flat. The rubbish was in plastic bags stacked outside and the floor had been swept. If I'd bought fly spray the place would've been almost habitable.

The big surprise was that Montefiore had taken the cast off and was massaging his leg, flexing his toes and going through a gentle rehab procedure. He seemed to know what he was doing and I was inclined to believe him about his martial arts prowess. He showered, washed his hair, shaved, put on his clean shirt, white jeans and sneakers and looked pale but capable of fending for himself.

I showed him the money and he nodded. 'You're a fucking life-saver.'

'I was, once.'

We had a beer and ate some of the food and tried to get on level terms. Not easy. We were wary of each other and both suspicious by nature.

'You didn't ask for cigarettes,' I said.

'I don't smoke, except the odd joint.'

I sniffed the air.

'Fay smokes. I can't stand the bloody things, but what can you do?'

He went out of the room again and I heard a few drawers open and close. When he came back he had a light blue linen jacket over his arm and was carrying a fair-sized overnight bag. 'Might have to move quick,' he said.

'What about the rent?'

'Fuck it.'

Just to make conversation, I said, 'You mentioned the plan to drop a small amount of heroin on Master. Turned out to be a couple of kilos and he went for ten minimum.'

Montefiore drained his can. 'No fridge,' he said. 'We either drink 'em or I put 'em in cold water in the sink.'

'I could go another one. It's pretty light. Keep two in hand. What d'you reckon about the drugs?'

We took cans from the pack and he went out to the kitchen and ran water. 'How could you trust those bastards?' he said when he came back. 'They double-cross everyone on principle.'

I cracked the second can and thought about it. 'How well did you know Master?'

He opened the can and put it aside. 'One's enough for now. I'm still thinking about getting a few head shots on Sione. Stewie? I'd never met him before. Gabe introduced him. I dunno. He'd clearly been around a bit. Couple of tatts that looked like gaol jobs, I noticed. Pretty quiet. Young looking, but I wouldn't have liked to mess with him. Seemed like he had something on his mind. Why?'

'Just something you said. I wonder if he was letting himself be set up for the drug bust. Say a minor one, for some reason, and they double-crossed him like you say.'

'You've lost me. Look, I'm going to take a nap. About four we can go to the place where Fay's working. They'll be rehearsing and we can talk to her about all this. You've got a car?'

'Yeah. Okay. Suppose this all goes well and I get the photo and you and Fay get the money, how would you get out? I've got the feeling Rivages could . . . intercept you.'

Montefiore stretched and yawned, obviously enjoying being free of the sling and cast. 'I've been thinking about that. Maybe on Reg's yacht.'

'All the way to Australia?'

'Nah. Vanuatu maybe. Money talks there, they tell me.'

Jarrod Montefiore was bouncing back, I judged—a player again.

We drove to the Salon de Fun. It was on the ground floor of a building that housed a restaurant on the first level and apartments above that. It wasn't far from the Île de France and the racetrack. Late afternoon shadows and overgrown bushes all but concealed the pathway to the joint, which looked as if it had once seen better days. The large windows were stained and mottled and a poor attempt had been made to blot out an old insignia and replace it with the new name. The old one still showed through and the replacement was amateurishly done. We stopped before reaching the doorway.

'Give me some money,' Montefiore said.

'How much?'

'As many ones as you can dig up.'

I fumbled among the cash in my pockets and couldn't help patting the money belt around my middle where I kept the serious stuff. I located seven or eight one thousand franc notes and handed them over. 'Comes off the top,' I said.

He grinned. 'Cheap bastard.' He was enjoying himself more by the minute.

The man standing by the door had a boxer's nose and a boozer's build. Montefiore spoke to him in rapid French, handed over a few notes and we were waved in. Inside, the place wasn't as bad as I'd expected. The floor was clean and the tables and chairs looked as if they got a regular wipe. The lighting wasn't bad and the stage wasn't the beer and sweat stained mess I'd seen in other strip joints. There were some of the standard props—the crotch pole, the tigerskin rug, the swing, the backboard with the manacles—all in reasonable condition. But no girls.

Montefiore walked across to the bar where a woman in a see-through blouse was wiping glasses. More fast French. She looked at her watch. 'Un moment,' she said and I understood that. Montefiore bought two beers and gave her a tip, something that wasn't usual in Noumea. She said something I couldn't catch but the name Fay was part of it.

The lights dimmed and the Kiwi Kuties trouped onto the stage. Unusual, I thought. One by one, getting hotter as they come on deck is the standard thing. We were standing well back from the lit-up stage and if the performers could see us they made no sign. Stripper music started blaring out and I saw right off that this was something different. The three women were all tall, leggy blondes with light tans. They wore satin blouses and loose silk trousers with very high heels. Red, white and blue with the odd star and stripe. As the music got going they began to gyrate, all keeping good time with some intricate steps, and to strip each other. They weaved around the stage, well choreographed, undoing buttons, sliding blouses off shoulders, letting silk pants whisper half down and toying with g-string ties and the fastenings of front-opening bras.

Suddenly, with an abrupt change in the rhythm of the music, this all changed and the performers went into their own routines, although they only mimed the actions so far— all that was needed, I supposed, in rehearsal.

'Good, aren't they?' Montefiore said and I fancied he was struggling to hold his heavy breathing in check.

'They are.'

'The one on the end's a bloke.'

'Which end?'

Montefiore snorted. 'Yeah, you'd never tell. Fay's in the middle. She's the best of them in my book.'

Fay certainly had all the attributes for the job and she seemed to be enjoying it. Montefiore moved forward into a patch of light and she stopped dead in the middle of a slither when she saw him.

'Jesus Christ, Jay.'

'Hi, babe.'

'What is this?' one of the others complained.

'I'm taking five.' Fay jumped down from the stage, landing with perfect balance on her high heels, and ran into Montefiore's waiting arms.

They hugged and kissed for a minute or two and then Montefiore introduced me. Dropping his voice, he said, 'He's got our ticket out of here—twenty-five grand. Right, Cliff?'

What she didn't know wouldn't hurt her until it wouldn't hurt me. I nodded and she gave me a hard look. 'For what?'

'Remember that creep who was hanging around and you got a snap of him?'

A yell came from the stage. 'Hey, Faysie, are we gonna do this or what?'

'Keep your gaff on, Rox. I'll be there in a minute. That much for the photo?'

'And information. You've still got it, haven't you? I told you it was insurance.'

'I think so.'

'*Think!* Jesus!'

'Don't fuckun' come uht wuth me, Jay.' Her accent thickened with anger. 'You got into this mess all on your own.'

'Twenty-five grand and out of this shithole,' Montefiore said. 'Sandy beaches and beer at three bucks a pop. A chance at some real money.'

'Yeah, with you puhmping me.'

'C'mon, babe.'

Montefiore was good. He had that quality a lot of women like, the quality that presumably attracted Lorraine to Stewart Master. Glen Withers, who'd shared the taste, told me about it once after we'd watched a video of *Chinatown*. Nicholson had it, she said, a bad twinkle in the eye.

'I'm pretty sure I know where it is. Have you seen the colour of his money?'

'Hey,' I said. 'I'm right here.'

'Yeah, sorry. You've got it.'

'I hand it over the minute I get the picture and a few details.'

She looked puzzled. 'Details?'

I looked at Montefiore, who made a gesture of resignation. 'I know you fucked him, Fay. Things were crook at the time.'

She was back doing it. 'So he wants to know how big his cock is?'

'I want a name and a close-up description of everything about him you can remember. Any paper you might have seen, phone call you might have heard. Anything.'

'Fay!'

'Coming. Right, we'll shoot over after the rehearsal. Three-quarters of an hour tops. Stay and watch the show.' She pecked Montefiore quickly on the cheek and danced back and up onto the stage, giving us a good look at her moving assets. We'd hardly touched our drinks and we both now took deep swigs.

'You think I'm nuts, don't you?'

'Mate,' I said, 'I don't know and I don't care. I'll just do my business with you both and then you can do as you please. You're not getting twenty-five though.'

He shrugged. 'Sweetening the pot. It's a habit. There's a public phone out front. Think I'll give the old Reg a call and see if I can set something up.'

'I'll take a walk on the beach.'

'It'll cost you to get back in.'

I shrugged. 'It's not my money, and it's not yours yet either.'

You don't leave Australia for beaches. The Ansa Vata beach was stony and gritty and the sand, what there was of it, was mud-coloured. The water looked good and the evening breeze had got up so that it wasn't such a bad place to be if only I hadn't been anxious about a number of things. Was Montefiore on the level? Would he have trouble dealing with Fay if he was? Could I stay out of their travel plans and how would I arrange my own? I sucked in the clean Pacific air and tried to tell myself that I'd done well and that everything was going to be all right. It never is.

Fay wore Montefiore's jacket over her stripper's outfit and she glided into the back seat of the car, pulling him in after her. She told me where to go and then they started whispering. I was surprised to hear her speaking French. There was more to Fay than I'd thought. Half a kilometre short of where we were heading she told me to pull up.

'Right here,' she said.

I stopped. You don't argue with a blonde stripper who speaks French. 'Why?'

'Old Jay here's a bullshitter from way back. You're not going to pay him twenty-five grand, are you?'

'Not quite.'

'How much? Really.'

'Like I said, depending on your information and the photo, maybe twenty.'

'I'll tell you what, Mr Detective—'

'Fay!'

'Shut up, Jay. It's twenty down and twenty when we get to Australia.'

'I don't know . . .'

'You want the name of the guy?'

'Sure.'

'I know it and a good bit more. Twenty in Sydney town and you get the lot.'

I swivelled around to look at her and she stared me straight in the eyes with her baby blues. Maybe contacts, but it made no difference. She was serious and she knew what she was doing. I couldn't help wondering if she knew more about the Master business than she was letting on. I told myself it could be useful to have her in Sydney, but maybe that was rationalisation. She had me over a barrel and she knew it.

'Okay,' I said. 'But Jarrod said you might be pissing off as soon as you got back to Australia.'

'Uh-uh. We'll stick around. I can smell the money in this.'

Clearly, she'd be calling the shots. I started the engine. 'Can we get this moving now?'

I heard her kiss Montefiore somewhere; at a guess, on the cheek. She was a card player. 'We're almost there, boys.'

Fay lived in a flat above a couple of up-market shops a kilometre or two back from the beach on one of the main arteries that wound its way towards the centre of town. She pointed to a spot on the street where I could park.

'Nothing off-street?' I said. 'Where's your spot?'

'Up you,' she said as she slid out. 'If I had enough money for a car d'you reckon I'd be tit-swinging here? We share this place. Roxy's screwing Carmel, sort of.'

'Jesus,' Montefiore said.

'Get over it, Jay. We all have to get along as best we can. What did kicking and belting people ever get you?'

He surprised me then by spinning slowly and slapping her quite hard. 'Respect,' he said.

She took it. She liked it. 'One more thing,' she said as she caressed the contact spot. 'Jay's talked to Reg Penny. He's waiting for the rest of your fuckin' money and now he's waiting for us. I'm packing a bag and we're off. Right?'

I had to admire her, but I had one more question. 'Who owns the Salon de Fun?'

'Who d'you reckon?' Montefiore said.

And the answer became obvious as we walked down the path towards the steps leading up to Fay's flat. A figure loomed up out of the shadows that was solid, not shadowy. Sione.

12

Fᴀʏ went straight to work. She slipped the jacket from her shoulders and marched up to Sione, all 'teeth and tits' as Mike Carlton said of Rose Hancock.

'Why, Sione, what're you doing here?'

She distracted him just long enough. Montefiore was right behind her, but he didn't go into his kick-boxing routine. He reached into the overnight bag and took out a pistol which he pointed at the bridge of the Polynesian's wide nose.

'Want something, cunt?'

'You.'

'Not this time.'

Montefiore had had the time and space to get nicely balanced and sighted. He feinted with his left and Sione's eyes followed it just long enough for Montefiore to crack him across the temple with the solid weight of the pistol. He caught him sweetly and the big man went down in a heap. Montefiore kicked him viciously in the ribs and he didn't move. He swung his foot back again but I stopped him.

'That'll do it. A cracked rib can puncture something else and you're up for murder. Let's get on with it.'

Fay was ahead of me. She dashed up the steps, worked her key and was into the flat in seconds. Montefiore followed and I stayed with Sione after making sure he had a strong pulse. There were only two other flats in the block and no activity around as the night got going. It wasn't a place where old folks sat around watching what went on.

It seemed longer, but it was probably only a couple of minutes until they came down the steps. Fay was wearing jeans, a T-shirt and sneakers and carrying a bag, and somehow she seemed all the more formidable without the glitz.

'I'm burning my bridges here, Cliffy' she said. 'You better have that fuckin' money.'

'He's got it,' Montefiore said. He was suddenly very confident and almost relaxed, carrying his bag in one hand and the pistol in the other. I had both hands free and I'd never have a better chance. I moved quickly, gripped the gun hand and twisted hard and down, slamming his fingers against the metal of the steps. The gun fell away and I grabbed it after one bounce. A Smith & Wesson .38 revolver. Good gun, knew it well. Oiled and loaded.

'You dumb fuck!' Fay shouted.

'Shut up! This can all go down okay for you, but I'll be buggered if it's going to happen with this thing floating around. Get him in the car. We'll drive to the dock. You'll get your money and I'll take it from there.'

Montefiore hated losing face in front of her but I hoped he could tell I'd use the gun if I had to. He gave it a few beats and I sweated.

'She can run you, Jay, if you like,' I said. 'But she's not going to run this whole bloody thing.'

'Fuck you,' Fay said.

I patted the money belt. I was sure Montefiore knew about it and that he'd told her while they were whispering in the back seat. I held the pistol steady. 'Jay?'

'You win, Hardy.'

'Keep it cool and we all win. I'll stick to the deal. Get him to the car and you can drive, Fay.'

She said something uncomplimentary I couldn't quite catch, but that's how it worked. We manhandled the unconscious Polynesian into the car. Fay, tightly strung, drove with me beside her and Montefiore and Sione in the back. She drove well and we were at the marina in quick time. I told Montefiore to fetch Penny.

'He wants his money too. Fay stays here.'

'Smart bastard, aren't you?' Fay said as Montefiore walked away with a bit of a limp.

'Fay,' I said, 'I hate to think how differently you would've choreographed this.'

She smiled her showgirl smile. 'You're right. Very duffrent.'

There was a certain amount of activity going on at the marina but nothing about what we were doing would attract attention. Penny and Montefiore returned and I got out of the car keeping the pistol held low.

'I told you to be careful,' Penny said. 'I told you he looked like a goer.'

Fay climbed out and stood beside Montefiore. 'You still haven't got the photo.'

'That's right,' I said. 'Let's be sensible about this. You want your money and I want the photo and to go in peace.'

'You wouldn't shoot here,' Montefiore said.

'Right. So do I just chuck it in the water?'

'Shit, no,' Montefiore yelped.

'Might not be a bad idea,' Penny said.

'Shut the fuck up, you two,' Fay said. 'I think he's trying to play it straight.'

I undid my shirt and lifted the flaps on several of the pockets of the money belt. I'd taken the precaution of putting precise amounts together in the compartments so I knew how much was where. I fished out the equivalent of four thousand and laid it on the bonnet of the car. 'That's yours, Reg. Nine all up.'

'You said ten.'

'There's a deduction for cooking up some scheme with Jay here to take me down.'

Penny shrugged and grabbed the money. I focused on Fay, who'd lit a cigarette. 'Photo.'

She produced it from the hip pocket of her jeans and smoothed it between her fingers.

'Show me.'

She held it up so that it caught the light. I could see a clear male image against a light background. 'Okay. What about twenty for you for the photo and the name and you walk away from these pricks here and now?'

I heard Montefiore gasp and Penny give a low, emphysemic chuckle.

Fay dropped her cigarette and stood on it. 'No.'

'Fair enough. Fifteen for the photo and twenty-five for the name and the other info in Sydney.'

'What's this?' Penny said.

'Shut up.' Fay slid the Polaroid across the bonnet and I did the same with the bundles of notes. She scooped them up and handed them to Montefiore.

'We're almost there,' I said, putting the photo in my shirt pocket. 'Got the boat ready, Reg?'

Penny nodded.

I gestured for them to move away and they obeyed, even though they knew I wouldn't use the gun. Guns are like that.

It was airless and warm down there in the port, and with the activity around the marina diminishing, our cluster would soon look noticeable. I was tired and stressed and sweating and wouldn't be able to keep this level of concentration up much longer. Also, I didn't know how close Sione might be to regaining consciousness.

I opened the driver's door and made sure Fay hadn't palmed the ignition keys. Sione hadn't moved. I nodded to Fay.

Best I could do. Dry-mouthed I said, 'See you in Sydney.'

'The gun,' Montefiore said.

I opened the cylinder, spilled the shells into my hand and tossed them to Penny. I flipped the pistol towards Montefiore and didn't care whether either of them made catches or not. I started the engine and drove slowly away.

There really wasn't much to think about. I drove to the hotel, parked as close to reception as I could and brought one of the flunkeys out to attend to Sione. While they were moving him and fussing about, I shifted the car. I raced up to my room, phoned the airport and was able to get on a plane leaving for Fiji in an hour and a half. I packed and quit the place with my bag slung over my shoulder, using the side steps, keeping out of sight. I figured Pascal Rivages could shout me a couple of breakfasts and a dinner.

The run to the airport was smooth at that time of night and I made it in forty-five minutes. I explained that I had to get to Fiji quickly and that my travel insurance would take care of the forfeited Noumea–Sydney flight. They looked me over fairly carefully and I sweated a bit, wondering how far Rivages' influence ran. Not far enough evidently, or he hadn't been put in the picture yet, because I caught the plane with a couple of minutes to spare.

The plane was half full and I had an empty seat next to me. My shirt was a damp rag and my feet hurt. The money belt itched. I took it off and stuffed it in my bag. I took my shoes off and spread myself, trying to relax after the high-adrenaline couple of hours I'd been through. I didn't think about Lorraine or Stewart Master, just about getting myself levelled out. It was a no-frills flight, no free French plonk this time. I made do with a couple of furtive, nerve-calming nips from the scotch in my cabin luggage.

I got out the Maugham stories and settled into a couple of my favourites—'Red' and 'The Fall of Edward Barnard'. Below me the mighty Pacific ocean was a blank stretch of nothing and when I'd calmed down I wondered how Jay and Fay and Reg were getting along out there on the good ship *You Beaut*.

13

WITH air fares, accommodation, expenses, my daily rates and what I'd paid Reg Penny and Jarrod Montefiore in Pacific francs, Lorraine Master had already shelled out a good deal in her husband's cause. I wanted to give her a full accounting by email plus an online copy of the photograph supplied by Fay Lewis, and a report on what I'd learned so far. All very cyber savvy, but the intrusive message on my computer suggested this would be very unsafe. Instead I phoned and stressed security. She was appreciative and issued an invitation to a business meeting over dinner at her home. Tomorrow night, which would make it two nights since I got home. Where were Jarrod and Fay? I wondered. Still at sea? I had no idea how long it'd take to sail from Noumea to Vila or even if that's where they'd gone. How good were Penny's engines and equipment now? How had Fay played her cards, and what about that .38?

Somehow, I had a feeling that before too long I'd meet up with Fay, at least, but how, where and when were anybody's guess. I made up for my misses at the Sunrise Surf's fitness gym by putting in two hard sessions at the Redgum. Even Wesley Scott commented on my dedication as I was leaving.

'You going to get serious, Cliff?'

'Semi-serious.'

'No such thing.'

'I know. Peter Lo been in?'

'Of course. Now there's serious.'

'He's young. I've had so many injuries over the years, a lot of places tweak and squawk.'

'Excuses, man, just excuses.' He glanced at the Air Calin bag I'd dumped my gym stuff in. 'Enjoy it over there? I guess not. No tan to speak of.'

'Work.'

He said something in rapid French. Maybe it was to do with Jacques and work and play but it was too quick for me to catch. That's Wesley. I wouldn't be surprised to hear him discussing Nietzsche in German.

Double Bay houses with water views probably start at around three million. Lorraine Master's place wasn't Paradis sur Mer, but it didn't seem to lack anything you might need. It was white, two-storey with a two-car garage, swimming pool, manicured garden and a view out over Seven Shillings Beach only partially interrupted by foliage and other buildings.

The wide driveway was closed by a high iron gate with a smaller entrance gate next to it. I parked in the street and buzzed.

'Cliff?'

'Yes.'

'Push.'

I did and the gate swung in. *Cliff?* I thought as I walked up a paved path to the front of the house. The garden beds were covered with some kind of straw and the trees and shrubs all looked healthy. Between the beds and under the trees was a low maintenance ground cover. I reflected that my front garden could look like this on a much smaller scale if I had a few grand to spend on it.

I went up a set of steps onto a tiled porch and got the button-pressing finger to work again. Butler? I thought. Filipina maid?

Lorraine Master opened the heavy interior door and released the catch on the solid security screen. She beckoned me in and then used the spare hand to invite me to shake. She was wearing a plain dress with a high neck and loose sleeves. Light blue. Suited her colouring. She had a small amount of jewellery about—neck chain, earrings—but it was unobtrusive and therefore probably cost a bomb. Her hand was dry and warm and I was reluctant to let it go. We went down a hallway, skirted a staircase and entered a room that murmured taste, money and comfort—things that don't always go together. Chairs upholstered in blue, pale grey carpet, well-filled bookshelves, track lighting and a drinks trolley.

'I'm going to have a g 'n t,' she said. 'You?'

'The same. Thanks.'

'Sit down. What's that you've got?'

I was holding a manilla folder with all the dope I hadn't been prepared to send online. I put in on the arm of the chair and settled down beside it. 'It's what you've paid for, so far. There's more to come.'

The level of Bombay gin rose to a commendable height in the glass. She dropped in a slice of lemon, two ice cubes and held up the tonic inquiringly. I put my thumb and fore-finger the right distance apart and she poured.

'More information or more money?'

'Both.'

'Okay.' She held out the glass and I had to reach to take it. I liked her style—classy and considerate, but not too considerate.

'Where're the kids?'

We did a quick silent toast. 'Why?' she said. 'Do you like kids?'

'I don't know many. Like some, not others.'

She sat and took a solid swig of a drink that looked to be about half the strength of mine. 'Ours are okay. They're upstairs. We've got an au pair. Why don't you drink your drink and let me read the report? I can't cook so I sent out for some food. Nothing special. We can discuss the details and whatever there is to discuss while we eat.'

I did as she'd done—extended the folder so that she had to lean forward from her chair to take it. She was the sort of woman you had to play those games with, otherwise, she'd have you in the back court all the time and you'd never make it to the net. The drink was just right for temperature, mix and punch and I sat back and enjoyed it while she read. I also enjoyed looking at her over the rim of the glass. Her skin glowed, her hair shone and her bones were well-covered. Whatever you've been up to, Stewart, I thought, you couldn't have expected her to wait ten years.

She read rapidly, flicking back to confirm things or lodge them in her memory, names perhaps. She was through it in a few minutes and then spent nearly half that long studying the photograph. She tapped the pages back together and pinned the photo back where it had been.

'Very professional,' she said. 'Let's eat.'

We went through to a dining room with a teak table that looked something like the one Paul Keating bought for the

Lodge. It was set for two places with a bottle of red wine standing by.

'I thought you'd be a meat man,' she said, 'so I ordered in some stuff from the Balkan. You know it?'

'I do. Great place. Haven't been there for a while. Still going strong?'

'Sure is. Wouldn't mind a percentage.' She picked up a waiter's friend style corkscrew and handed it to me. 'Open the wine while I bring in the food. Freshen your drink if you like.'

I did both things. I could hear sounds from the kitchen—microwaving, a fridge door, the rattle of plates. She came back with a stack of plates and a couple of steaming bowls on a tray, set them down and went back for more. After another trip we sat down to a spread of oysters in the shell, skewered meat with vegetables and rice, breadsticks and side dishes of spiced sausages and various sauces and dips I couldn't name. The solid gins had relaxed me and the wine was smooth and fruity. We both dug in for a minute or two and then she looked across at me with a forkful held ready.

'What's wrong?' she said.

'I was thinking of Stewart.'

The fork clattered to the table and the food spilled. 'Fuck you,' she said.

'Sorry.'

She had the fastest recovery time I'd ever seen. She had the spilt food scooped up and back on her plate, her lips wiped with a napkin and had taken a sip of wine before I could think of the next thing to say.

'Just sometimes,' she said, 'I try to forget that my husband's facing ten years in gaol and that I've got two kids to explain things to and a business to run and—'

'Let's start again,' I said. 'It was very nice of you to invite me and I'm enjoying it. Let's talk about something else. Yachting. How long for a yacht to go from Noumea to Vila?'

She gave her throaty laugh. 'You bastard, that's not something else. You're still working. Am I being rude?'

I knew she was manipulative, but was she *that* manipulative? Hard to say. 'You're doing fine, most women'd be climbing the walls. Most *people*.'

'Caught yourself almost in time.'

'Old habits. The food's great.' I reached over and poured her some more wine. We ate and drank for a few minutes, both things she did neatly and efficiently. She seemed to enjoy the wine without wanting to get it down as fast as possible, but it's hard to tell with drinking. I knew a bloke who I'd have said drank about as much as me and ended up going to AA. I said if he did maybe I should but he told me he usually had half a bottle of scotch inside him before we got together and finished off the rest later.

She pushed her plate away and had a good sip. 'Right. So where are we? Some kind of a policeman set Stewart up.'

'If we can believe Fay and Montefiore.'

'Mmm. Which one was she?' I'd put the Salon de Fun leaflet in the folder.

'She was the one on the end.'

'Which end?'

'That's what I asked Montefiore.'

She smiled. 'You sort of liked them, didn't you? D'you believe them?'

'I've met worse. Chancers, toughies. We'll see if they turn up with some solid information. If they don't, you've spent a fair bit of money for nothing.'

'I think you handled it well. You baited the hook. Is there anything to be done while we wait?'

I drank some more wine, judging it to be about five notches in quality above the stuff I'm used to. 'It's difficult. If he is a policeman he could be federal or from any one of the eastern states. Very hard to find out if he's an undercover type. I'll have to talk more to Fay to get a line on that. If he isn't . . .'

'Is that worse or better?'

I broke a breadstick and poked it into one of the sauce bowls. 'I'll be honest with you, Mrs Master—'

'Lorrie.'

'Okay, Lorrie. I just don't know. I haven't come up against anything quite like this before. Rogue cops, yes. High level, complex international operations, no.'

'Isn't there some kind of internal affairs department in the police?'

'Yes, but which state, and state or federal? Same problem.'

'Let's leave that aside for a moment. I'm interested in a sly suggestion you made—that Stewart might have agreed to cooperate with . . . whoever, and got double-crossed.'

I shrugged. 'It was just a thought. No, more like a feeling. I had a sense of him perhaps walking into a situation with his eyes open.'

'How could that be?'

Something about her concentrated alertness made me want to fidget, to play with the breadstick, spin my wineglass. I kept my hands still. 'What if Stewart was into something here that went badly wrong and the cops had him over a barrel? So he had to agree to a part in this sting or whatever it was, or they'd hit him with everything.'

She shook her head confidently. 'No. That's not possible. He'd broken off all his ties with the crims. He didn't
have any money but he wasn't looking to get it in the old
way. He was happy to lie low, think about things, get himself
back in order. He was considering doing a university course.
Psychology. Becoming some sort of counsellor—'

She broke off and stared at me. 'Why are you looking
like that?'

'Did you know he'd put in an offer to buy the Atlas gym?'

14

'THAT bastard!'

She slammed her glass down so hard that the base and stem broke and red wine spilled out over the white tablecloth. Not content with that, she hammered her fist on the table and let out a stream of obscenities directed at men in general and Stewart Henry Master in particular. 'He promised me,' she snarled. 'He fucking promised! No more scams. No more dodgy deals. Shit! That's it. I'm finished. He's had it. He can fucking rot in there as far as I'm concerned, the lying prick!'

Nothing to do except sit quietly and wait for the storm to pass. It didn't. She reeled off a list of betrayals and deceptions Master had perpetrated and castigated herself for her forgiving ways.

'No more. It's finished.' She glared at me and it was clear that I'd gone from helpful employee or something more to less than nothing. I heard a movement outside the room and a pretty young head poked around the door.

'Mrs Master . . .?'

'Go away, Britt. Go away!'

The head withdrew and Lorraine Master continued to rage, sweeping things from the table and almost spitting as she spoke.

'Ten years. It should be twenty. The lying . . .'

That was enough. I took out my keys and rattled them in her face. 'Stop it. It might not be as bad as you think.'

'That's all you know,' she spat. 'This is a typical piece of Stewie bullshit. He must've done some kind of deal to come out of this New Caledonia thing with money and it all went sour on him. Good. Fuck him!'

She meant it. She was the clean-sweep queen and she was holding all the cards. I hadn't expected the news about the gym buy to trigger this much reaction but I wasn't completely surprised. Master was a conman; Lorraine was the kind of woman vulnerable to that kind of man. Neither of them could help themselves. It was time to think of number one.

'Where does that leave me, Lorrie?'

She caught the sarcasm and it didn't faze her one bit. She jumped up, went out and returned with her shoulder bag. She dug out her jumbo-sized cheque book, flipped quickly through the manilla folder and wrote a cheque which she put on the table within my reach.

'Our business is finished.'

I ignored the cheque. 'Your privilege,' I said. 'What about Montefiore and his girlfriend?'

'Turn them over to the police. And now, if you don't mind, I'd be glad if you left. I have some thinking to do.'

I got up, folded the cheque and put it away and knocked off the rest of my wine. 'You know where to contact me if you change your mind.'

'I won't.'

I left. She was genuinely distressed and I was pretty sure she'd paid enough for me to let her have the last word.

. . .

It's not often a case blows up in your face quite that suddenly and completely. I drove home in a slightly stunned state. I realised I'd become involved in the Master case to an unusual degree and not just because of the intrigue and mystery attached to it. It was all very well for Lorraine to tell me to turn Jay and Fay over to the cops. It wasn't that easy. Charging them with what? I was their first port of call, always supposing they made it back. They weren't pushovers and it was hard to say what frame of mind they'd be in. It depended on how things had gone since I waved them goodbye. They'd have high expectations. Very sticky.

I've had clients pull out before for one reason or another and even a couple die in the middle of proceedings. In those cases you're inevitably short-changed, sometimes stiffed altogether. Not with our Lorraine. Her cheque covered every-thing I'd run up on my credit cards, paid me for more days than I'd put in and if I cashed in the return flight from Noumea I'd be well ahead. I could use the money, but it gave me an uneasy feeling. I like closure, hate loose ends. There was no way in the world Jay and Fay were going to get twenty-five grand from me. I realised I was starting to think of them as an act, almost a comic turn, and that was dangerous.

The next day I banked the cheque and paid some bills and tried to feel good about that. Over the next couple of weeks I dealt with routine matters—served writs, body-guarded a corporate high flyer whose business had gone west so that he had more enemies than Rasputin. Nothing happened and he grew in confidence by the minute so that after three days he reckoned he didn't need me any more. I wasn't sorry to be released, another day of his bragging bullshit and I'd have pushed him out of a window. I heard nothing from Mrs M.

Then Bali happened and everyone went security crazy as the government and the media played it for all it was worth and more. The phone never stopped ringing with requests for debugging, escorts for school children of diplomats, an armed presence at functions, security training for corporate personnel. I handled it personally as much as I could and off-loaded it to other PEAs when I couldn't. I met a lot of people from different walks of life, of different nationalities, all united in fear. It was a circus and in my more cynical moments I felt I could smell the orchestration, the political opportunism, the massaging of the worst human impulses. But I made money and began to think about a break, some time out from human dishonesty.

Then Lorraine Master rang me.

'They've contacted me, Mr Hardy.'

What happened to Cliff? I thought, but I said, 'Tell me.'

'A phone call to the office. A demand for twenty-five thousand dollars.'

'Him or her?'

'Him. Jarrod Montefiore.'

'Have you ever met him? I got the impression from the letters that you knew some of the people Stewart mentioned.'

'Only Reg Penny, through the yachts. Possibly Gabriel Rosito, I'm not sure. No, I never met Montefiore and I don't want to. He was very demanding, very threatening. I thought . . .'

'You thought they'd contact me and I'd have to handle it somehow. After all, I gave the undertaking.'

'Yes.'

'And now?'

I was in my office late in the day with the city slowly going quiet around me. I had money in the bank and no

big bills and I'd lost a couple of kilos through keeping
busy and hard workouts. I didn't need any complications
and I could feel one heading towards me from the long
pause at the end of the line. Lorraine Master wasn't one for
long pauses. 'God,' she said. 'I don't know. It's so hard
without him. Jasper keeps asking about him. He's two,
almost three. He's very bright and he's bound to find out
before long. He'll want to visit him and Stewart won't
allow it. God . . .'

'What about the other child?'

'Inez? She's six. She's Lance's. She adores Stewart. Lance
is a write-off. Can't blame him, he didn't want a child. She's
become too clinging. It's a mess.'

'Where's this heading, Mrs Master?'

Her sigh came down the line like a harsh wind. 'I won't
have him back. I know I can't trust him. But if he was out at
least the children wouldn't suffer. We could work something
out. I could help him set up a business or something. Maybe
it wouldn't be too bad.'

She was talking to herself rather than to me and clearly
she'd been doing it for some time. I felt like a psychiatrist
letting the patient talk and then saying, 'And what do *you*
think about that?' I tried to take a different tack.

'Have you talked to anyone else about this? I mean the
problem with the kids?'

'No. Who would I talk to?'

'I don't know. A doctor. Friends?'

The pause again. 'I haven't got any friends.'

I could tell she was speaking the truth and suddenly I
saw her life in a different light—the big house, the au pair,
the yacht, the gym, the office, the wealthy clients, Fiona the
champion diver, the Tom Cruise lookalike underling and

bugger-all else. I could feel myself being drawn back into it and I didn't want to go.

'What about the lawyer, O'Connor?'

'I spoke to him as soon as I started thinking this way. Before Montefiore phoned. He says he can't see a way to get Stewart out early.'

'Has he told Stewart?'

'I imagine not. He doesn't like dispensing bad news.'

'No one does, Mrs Master.'

'I know, but here's some for you, Mr Hardy. I want to re-employ you. I want you to pay this creep his money and get the information he has and use it to get my husband released. I'll pay you whatever you ask.'

15

WHAT do you say? To knock it back would seem like handing in my ticket and taking up another line of work. No way. It crossed my mind that I hadn't had any unpleasant messages on my computer or been knocked down stairs in the dark since Lorraine's cancellation. Could I expect that to start again? But then I had to admit I was interested to see how things had worked out with Jay and Fay and Reg. And at least this time I'd be dealing with them on my own turf.

'Mr Hardy?'

I'd been silent for too long. 'Okay,' I said. 'I'll take it on, but you know how things stand. How tricky it all is. There are no guarantees.'

'There never are. I learned that a long time ago. Thank you. As to the money . . .'

'You've already paid me enough money to get started. We'll see how it goes. We'd better meet and you can fill me in on all the details.'

'Right. I can be there in a couple of minutes. I'm on my mobile. I'm parked in William Street.'

I had to laugh. 'Jesus, you were confident.'

'No. I was desperate.'

St Peters Lane, even though the area is gentrifying fast, isn't a place to walk around in after dark, for man or woman. I went down and waited for her at the door. The bonnet of a silver Saab appeared at the top of the lane and stopped in a marginally legal parking spot. A bit of a parking fine wouldn't worry Lorraine and the attendants gave the area a wide berth anyway. I heard the door close and then she was striding down the middle of the strip. I was starting to learn to read her. Would she have the white suit on? Sexy and successful. Or the smart dress, neutral colour? Relaxed and in control. Neither. She was in dark pants, dark shirt, blazer, flatties. All business.

It was cold there in the shadows and I was in shirtsleeves. I have to admit it—the sight of her warmed me. She stopped a metre away, shifted her bag on her shoulder.

'Mrs Master.'

'Can we go back to Lorrie?'

'Didn't work so well last time.'

'I'm sorry. I didn't behave well.'

'Lorrie, it is. Let's go up; it's cold down here. I can't offer you anything like the hospitality you offered me.'

'Don't worry about it. I saw your set-up and I'd settle for a cup of instant. I sat there in the car for over an hour trying to summon up the courage to ring you.'

'I'm glad you did,' I said, and I meant it.

Had to hand it to her. She had the answering machine tape of Montefiore's first message, the one she hadn't been home for. She made notes on the second message and she recorded the third.

'Mrs Master, I met your detective Hardy in Noumea. We have some unfinished business. I'll call again.'

The next time he rang he made remarks about the monkey and the organ-grinder. He said he expected she'd use me as a go-between, which was all I ever was. He'd give her a day or two to contact me and then he'd call again with instructions.

'Mrs Master, why do I suspect you're recording this? But I do. I hope you're planning to cooperate. I'll ring Hardy on his mobile soon and I'll expect you to have made arrangements with him. I understand your reluctance to talk to me. I'm not offended. Goodbye.'

'Pretty slick,' I said. 'No names, no threats, but it's interesting that he's being so cautious. This isn't extortion. I think on the whole it's a good sign.'

'Why?' I'd made two mugs of instant coffee with long-life milk and she was drinking hers with what looked like enjoyment.

'It suggests that the information is genuine. That the guy in question really is a cop, straight or crooked, and that they're in dangerous waters. Chances are they could be in some trouble themselves.'

'Like?'

I drank the coffee which tasted fine to me, though not as good as the stuff in Noumea. 'I don't know. Problems with Penny? Problems between the two of them? Outstanding warrants? Illegal entry?'

'I'm not interested in getting the upper hand, Cliff. When he rings, I just want you to agree to his terms and get the name and anything else on offer. We can take it from there.'

I nodded. 'Let's hope it goes that way.'

'What else?'

'Someone doesn't want this looked into. What if Montefiore's playing both sides of the street?'

'Mmm. Is that likely?'

'It's possible. What if he's been out to see Stewart?'

She almost jumped from her lumpy chair. 'Why d'you say that?'

'Just speculating. What's wrong?'

She relaxed back in the chair and wrapped her hands around the mug as if the warmth would comfort her. 'I went to see him the other day.'

'What did you tell him?'

'Everything. He was furious. Told me not to interfere and that he'd sort it out himself. I lost my temper. Well, you've seen what that's like. I argued with him about the gym purchase. We ended up shouting at each other and he walked out.'

'But you still want to . . .'

She nodded vigorously. That gesture had made her glossy hair bounce the previous time. Now the hair was less glossy, less alive. She seemed to have aged a bit. In a way it made her more attractive. The artificiality I'd noticed in her features previously had diminished. It must have been a matter of makeup and deliberate control of facial muscles. Now the makeup was less careful and distress had removed some of the control. She drained her mug and set it on the desk.

'I've made a mess of two men's lives, I don't want the score to go up to three. I still want to help him.'

'Even if he doesn't want you to.'

'Yes.'

'Does you credit, Lorrie. Well, we'll see how it goes when Montefiore rings. These sort of elaborate entrapments have a way of going wrong. I suppose if we can find out enough we can apply some pressure in the right places. Maybe threaten to go to the media. Who knows? But it's still a long shot.'

She gave me a searching look and the strain lines subsided as she smiled. 'That's not what you mean, Cliff. You mean it's dangerous.'

'Yeah. Could be. For all concerned. Stewart included.'

She shrugged. 'I'm game and my guess is you are as well. Stewart? He doesn't have any choice.'

It wasn't a bad summary of the situation—realistic, pragmatic. She stood and I did too, as a sort of reflex action. She moved around the desk and I found myself moving towards her. We stood close, almost touching. She drew in a deep breath and I saw her full breasts rise inside her shirt. She lifted her left hand and stroked the right side of my bristled face. I hadn't noticed that she was left-handed. Some detective. Her hand was warm.

She stepped back. 'Sorry. Sorry. Not a good idea. Shit, I didn't mean to . . .'

I reached, took hold of her hand again, held it for a few seconds, lowered it and let it go. 'I like the idea.'

'No. Not now. Let's . . .'

We'd got through the moment, just, and we both knew it. 'Right,' I said. 'You'd better get back to Britt and the kids and I'd better make sure my mobile's charged up. Things to do. I'll see you to your car, Lorrie. No harm in that.'

She smiled. 'No harm at all.'

Montefiore's call came through later that night.

'Hardy? This is Jay Montefiore.'

'I've been expecting you.'

'That right? Good. Means the lady with the loot's been taking notice.'

'Speak your piece.'

'Don't you want to hear about our voyage?'

'All I want to hear is where I meet up with Fay and when and how I make sure you're not both bullshitting.'

'Yeah? How d'you reckon to do that?'

Unbidden, an idea came into my mind. I said: 'I'll have someone with me who's an expert on analysing testimony. She'll record what Fay says and examine it. When and if she's satisfied, you'll get your money.'

There was a long silence. 'Jesus. I don't know about that.'

'Take it or leave it. How's Reg?'

'What the fuck d'you care?'

'I don't much. Just thinking out loud. Mrs Master knows him and that counts for something. I thought Fay had an eye for him and he didn't wave a gun at me. I'm wondering if we really need you in the picture, Jay.'

'You're a tricky bastard, Hardy, but it won't work. Sucked in—Penny's gay, didn't you notice?'

I had, sort of. 'Just trying to get you going, but what I say still holds. Two of us, two of you. A tape. A couple of hours. Then you get your payday. When're you getting married?'

'Fuck you. I'll ring later.'

He hung up and I closed the mobile with a grin on my face. It never hurts to keep the opposition off balance. Worth a drink. I poured a moderate scotch and added a few millilitres of water. I had a candidate in mind for the testimony analysis.

The phone rang again before I'd done much damage to the drink. I picked it up and didn't speak.

'Hardy?'

'You're back.'

'Don't be more of a smartarse than you can help. Okay, we agree to your terms. The meet's tomorrow, nine sharp. Here's the address—flat three, 213a Darling Street, Balmain.'

I made a note, even though I was recording the call. 'Why there?'

'This isn't a fuckin' chitchat. That's it.'.

'At a guess, Penny's boat's moored nearby.'

'Fuck you.'

'You sound anxious, Jay.'

'I'm anxious to get the money. That's all.'

'Can I talk to Fay?'

'No.'

'Why not?'

'Stop pissing around.'

'Okay. You don't imagine I'm going to waltz in with twenty-five thousand cash in my briefcase, do you?'

'You better.'

'Get real. You're green as grass at this game, Jay. I've done it before. In this country, every bank transaction of ten thousand dollars and over gets reported to the authorities. Mrs Master's going to have to make three withdrawals from three different accounts. She can't make them between now and nine o'clock tomorrow. Maybe you'd like to take cheques?'

'Jesus, if I was there, Hardy, I'd—'

'I'm sure you would. You're not old and you're a kick-boxer. I've never understood that sport, if that's what it is. Kicking was considered cowardly when I was growing up.'

He let out a stream of obscenities and I realised that he was pretty drunk. There was the sound of a whispered exchange, then an altercation at the end of the line and a different voice cut through: 'Hardy? This is Fay. What're you playing at?'

'Welcome to Australia, Fay. Nothing, really, just trying to ensure a level playing field.' I repeated what I'd said to Montefiore about the money. Fay didn't rant and rave.

'You listen to me, Hardy. You'd better turn up with five grand minimum or it's no deal. Your client should be able to lay her hands on that much one way or another between now and then. If she can't, she's probably not going to come up with the rest. You tell her that. You tell her as soon as this call ends. And don't bother with the call-back number. We won't be there.'

Fay was the real player and the one with the savvy. 'All right, Fay,' I said. 'That's one for your team. But I've got one more condition.'

'I'm running out of patience here. What?'

'I'll want to see that .38 sitting somewhere in plain view, unloaded, with the cylinder open.'

'You're paranoid.'

'Big word. D'you know what it means?'

End of call.

16

IPHONED Lorraine and gave her the story. She asked why I'd played so hard to get and I told her I didn't like being dictated to and that, with people like this, you had to keep an edge. And that I had another reason.

'What's that?'

'I thought you might like to come along—as this non-existent testimony analyser.'

'At nine o'clock in the morning in Balmain? Have you any idea what my day is looking like tomorrow?'

'It was just a thought. You're shelling out a lot of money. I thought you deserved a chance to look at where it's going. As well as that, I think you probably are a good judge of character, with the occasional slip, and you might be better able to judge the value of what Fay says than me.'

'You really think that?'

'I do.'

'No ulterior motive?'

'How d'you mean?'

'I can guess what you think of me, Cliff. That I'm one of those women attracted to bad men. Like the helicopter lady, right?'

'It crossed my mind.'

'Maybe you're the same. Attracted to women with bad track records with men. Bitches.'

'I wouldn't say that.'

'Jesus, as if I haven't got enough worries. But what if they know me? What if someone's been watching me, or Penny's given them a description?'

'Good point. Got a wig? Four-inch heels?'

She gave a snort of amusement. 'I'll be there. Wouldn't miss it. How much money should I scrape up?'

'Four thousand.'

'I thought you said five.'

'Stuff them.'

She laughed and we agreed to meet in Balmain a few minutes before the appointed time. I'd be there earlier but I didn't tell her that.

I realised I still had half of the drink I'd made when Montefiore's first call came through. I hadn't touched it through the second call or when talking to Lorraine. I freshened it up and sat back. What are you doing? I thought. The woman's ripped the heart out of two weak men and she's prepared to go to bat for a third strong one only so he can co-parent for her. Keep your professional and emotional distance. I hadn't even liked her at first. But then, I hadn't liked Cyn with her North Shore ways straight off, or Helen Broadway with her divided loyalties, or Glen Withers, imbued with the police culture. I drank the scotch and wrestled with the thought that maybe Lorrie Master was right—I was attracted to unsuitable women. If so, too bad.

. . .

Montefiore bunched a fist. 'I said five.'

I shrugged. 'All she could muster.'

Fay butted her cigarette and dropped heavily into a chair. 'Sit down, Jay. What the fuck's the difference?'

Montefiore glanced at the .38.

'Don't even think it,' I said. 'You've got twenty thousand eight hundred and fifty dollars to come.'

He sat down next to Fay. 'It'd be almost worth it, you tricky cunt.'

Lorrie glanced at me. 'Can we start, Mr Hardy? I've got a busy day.'

Fay lit another cigarette. The air in the room, already stale and smelly, was thickening. 'I thought you were going to record this,' she said.

I nodded. 'We're recording. Let's start with the bloke's name. Make it loud and clear.'

'She's not even listening,' Fay said.

Annoyed, I glanced at Lorrie, who was looking distracted. 'She'll listen to the tape.'

'I can hear something outside,' Lorrie said. 'I—'

The flimsy door crashed inwards and a man wearing a stocking mask burst through the gap. He had a pistol with a long barrel in his hand and he fired twice quickly, the shots no louder than heavy coughing. I pulled Lorrie to the floor between the first and second reports and Montefiore, who'd been hit somewhere low, reeled towards the gunman, who shot him again, point-blank. I scrabbled across the carpet to the television set, bumped it away stand and all with my shoulder and scooped up the .38, praying that it was loaded. Montefiore had collapsed towards the gunman but was still clutching at him. The gunman squeezed off more wild shots before I had the .38 roughly aligned. I fired twice in his direction but he was already moving, heaving against Montefiore's bulk, heading for the door. I fired again, but he was gone.

The air in the room was thick with the smell of cordite and dust from where the bullets had impacted on the walls and ceiling. I coughed and spluttered as I got to my feet, fighting for physical and mental balance. Through the haze I could see that Fay was lying back in her chair, a dark hole in the middle of her forehead. Montefiore lay face down with his hands stretched out like claws, pointing in the direction his killer had taken. Blood from his wounds had surged forward and was trickling towards the shattered door.

'Lorrie?'

I dived down under the table where I'd pulled her and found her on her back, staring up at the holes that had punched through the Formica. She was breathing, but a dark stain was still spreading across her pale blue blouse.

17

THEN it was chaos, ambulances, cops and more cops. Fay was dead and Montefiore was close to it. Lorrie had a serious shoulder wound and I was unhurt apart from a pain in the shoulder damaged in my earlier fall downstairs and again in the flat, so all the shit came down on me. I gave them the names of the dead, dying and wounded and my own name. They bagged the .38 and the money and would have taken the tape recorder if they'd found it. Then they hauled me off to College Street, gave me a few minutes to use the toilet and set to work. Detective Inspector Keith Carmichael, forty plus and beefy, was ably assisted by Detective Sergeant Lucille Hammond, lean, dark and keen.

I agreed to be interviewed without a legal representative present but reserved the right to call one in if I chose. Then I refused to say anything until I established that Lorraine Master's lawyer and the au pair had been informed and that arrangements were in place to look after the children.

'She's okay, Hardy,' Carmichael said. 'Small calibre flesh wound. No bone damage. Clean exit. Shock and blood loss. That's it.'

'Thanks,' I said. 'Montefiore?'

Carmichael shook his head. 'Took five rounds to stop him. Small calibre, like I say. He was unlucky, one nicked the aorta.'

'He had some guts. He kept trying.'

'Like you?' Hammond said.

I shook my head. It was still early but the adrenaline rush had faded, leaving me worn and tired. 'No. I just blasted away a couple of times.'

'Scared him off, but,' Carmichael said.

'If you say so. Anyone see him?'

Hammond consulted her notebook. 'Yeah, and lucky for you.'

'How's that?'

'Otherwise it might look like you did it.'

'Right. What did I do with the pistol and the silencer?'

She shrugged. 'It's not an issue. A couple of people saw a man running along Darling Street not long after the shots. That'd be *your* shots. Went through Gladstone Park and then . . .' She closed the notebook.

Carmichael nodded to her and she switched on the tape recorder and logged the date and time and the names and credentials of those present.

'Okay, Hardy,' Carmichael said. 'Let's hear it.'

From long established habit, I stuck to the truth as much as I could and tried not to include or exclude anything that might contradict Lorrie's version. I said that Mrs Master had hired me to investigate the circumstances of her husband's conviction and that I'd gone to Noumea, met Fay Lewis and Jarrod Montefiore and arranged to pay them money for information back in Sydney. When they asked what the information was, I told them it was the name of an individual they suspected of some involvement.

'And that name was?' Carmichael asked.

I shook my head. 'Fay Lewis knew the name but she was shot before she could tell us.'

'And you've no idea?'

'All I know is that someone left a threatening message on my computer soon after my first meeting with Mrs Master and that I was attacked about the same time.'

Hammond said, 'Attacked?'

'I was knocked down a set of stairs.'

From the looks on their faces they would both have been happy to do the same, now or sometime in the future. 'C'mon, Hardy,' Carmichael growled, 'you know more than that.'

I did, sort of. But there was no chance I'd tell them about Montefiore's version of the conspiracy to convict Master and the alleged police involvement in getting a big haul of marijuana onto the Australian market. I had no idea whether the story was true, but if it was, a couple of New South Wales cops I knew nothing about weren't the people to talk to.

'All I know is that an average-sized man, or maybe a tallish woman, wearing dark clothes and a stocking mask killed Fay Lewis and Montefiore and would've killed Mrs Master and me except that I got lucky.'

'Bullshit,' Hammond said.

I shrugged. 'Ask Mrs Master.'

Carmichael snuffled and blew his nose. 'Oh, we will. And we'll jump through any cracks in your stories.'

'You'd better be careful. She's a very successful high-powered businesswoman and she's got a top-flight lawyer.'

Carmichael blew his nose again and Hammond drew slightly away from him. 'She's married to a lowlife.'

'I wouldn't say that.'

She jumped at it. 'So you've met Master? That's interesting.'

I hadn't meant to let that slip, but it wasn't disastrous. 'I saw him out at Avonlea after I took this case on.'

'You didn't know him before that?'

'No.'

'Or Mrs Master?'

'No.'

'How well do you know her now?'

'What do you mean?'

Carmichael took over. 'You know what she means. You saved her fucking life, it looks like.'

'And mine, don't forget. Where is she, by the way?'

'By the way,' he mocked. 'She's down the road in Balmain hospital, but if what you say's right, she'll be in some flash private place any minute.'

Hammond said, 'Where did the gun come from?'

'It was there.'

'Whose was it?'

'No idea.'

'You knew how to use it.'

'I've got one similar. Licensed. But I didn't have it with me.'

'You weren't expecting trouble?'

The air in the interview room was stale and Carmichael was filling it with germs. My chair was hard and my eyes were still stinging from the cordite and plaster dust. 'Look, I'm getting tired of this. I've been cooperative and tried to tell you everything I know. I've got a client in hospital, a car collecting fines and a shoulder that hurts like buggery. I've also got a solicitor. Do we wind this up for now, or do I contact him?'

Carmichael burst into a fusillade of sneezing and coughing and his high colour got even higher. Hammond looked concerned and when he caught his breath he gave her the nod.

'Interview concluded at 11.50 am,' she said and turned off the machine. 'And you're a slippery prick, Mr Hardy.'

I suppressed a rude reply.

I took a taxi back to Balmain and found my car sitting on its wheel rims with the tyres slashed. A heavy parking fine and an unroadworthy notice completed the picture. I organised an NRMA tow, watched SOC officers at work behind their blue and white tape up at the flats, and then went into the convenience store for some painkillers and on to the Gladstone for a long overdue drink.

Over the beer, with the paracetamol cutting in to dull the pain in my shoulder, I reflected on what had happened and how things stood. The police didn't believe me but there wasn't much they could do about it. The four thousand dollars plus wasn't a lot of money, not enough to positively contradict my story. That might change if they found a sizeable amount of the money I'd paid out to Montefiore and Fay in Noumea lying around in their flat, but somehow I doubted they would. Those two were the type to spend it and stash it.

I'd described the gunman accurately to the police, which is to say hardly at all. The quick look I'd had at him was consistent with what I'd been told about the Noumea mystery man, but it also fitted about eighty per cent of the Australian adult male population. The name was further from our grasp than before. But maybe not completely out of reach. There was a chance that Reg Penny knew it, just a chance. A better than even chance of knowing lay with Stewart Master, but he wasn't likely to cough it up. The 'man without a name' was in Sydney; he knew my car and office and probably my house. Did he know Lorrie? Hard to say.

I had a second beer and a toasted sandwich and felt more or less composed. I'd left my mobile in the car. I used the hotel's public phone to call Bryce O'Connor and was put straight through to him.

'This is a mess, Hardy.'

'Could be worse. Lorraine and I could be dead. Or maybe you wouldn't consider that worse.'

A pause. 'I don't get your meaning.'

'Forget it. I'm stressed. The cops say she's probably gone from Balmain hospital by now. Where is she?'

'I'm not sure I should tell you. What in God's name has been going on?'

'I could fill you in, I suppose, if you dropped the outraged manner and cooperated. A very dangerous person is out there. It's all to do with Stewart Master's conviction—a cooked-up job. You're involved at that point. Then there's my investigation and who knows how wide it could spread? We've got a dead man in Noumea and two dead people here in Sydney. And a wounded woman—your client and mine. This goes beyond the legal niceties, *Mr O'Connor.* Where the fuck is she?'

'She's in the Cartland private hospital in Bellevue Hill. I thought she should be near her business associates and her children.'

'Very thoughtful. I hope you arranged for security.'

'I did. There's a guard.'

'Good. Contact him and authorise access for me on proof of identity.'

'Why should I?'

'Because if you don't, Bryce, when all this gets sorted out, and it will, I'll tell how you helped to set Stewart Master up for a gaol stretch he didn't really earn.'

'You're being ridiculous, but I'll make the call and Lorraine can deal with you herself. What possessed you to take her to this criminal meeting I can't imagine. I'll be surprised if she doesn't report you to whatever sleazy authority supposedly regulates your profession.'

'Nice speech. Good stuff in court, but it sounds like bullshit to me.'

He hung up. Accusing him was a shot in the dark and I couldn't tell whether it had struck home or not. He was a smooth one, possibly worth his price whoever paid. I rang the Cartland and was told that Mrs Master was sleeping peacefully. The nurse brought the guard to the phone and he confirmed that O'Connor had rung him. He sounded young, alert and American.

'Please ask when it'd be possible for me to see her,' I said. I heard some murmuring and then he came back on the line.

'They say later today, around five o'clock.'

'Thanks, I'll see you then. You are . . .?'

'Hank Bachelor. Mr Hardy, what exactly is the threat here?'

'Look out for a guy in a stocking mask with a silenced pistol,' I said.

The Cartland was as unlike the Victorian piles that house most of our public hospitals as it was possible to be. In fact, with its tinted glass and white bricks and landscaping, it reminded me of the Atlas gym. Lorrie was in a private room of course, on the third floor, no doubt with a view.

Hank Bachelor had the size and the physical presence for his job and the boredom that kind of work entails hadn't yet taken its toll on him. He watched my approach carefully with his hand on something nestling in his lap. I stopped a few metres away and said my name.

He nodded and I went closer. He put his piece of equipment on the chair and stood. He shook my hand vigorously, told me that 'the lady' was looking forward to seeing me, and that he aspired to be a private enquiry agent himself. He was doing the TAFE course.

'Interesting work, huh?'

'It can be, but there's also a lot of this sort of sitting around and waiting.'

He looked crestfallen but only for a moment. He had that buoyant Yank attitude they graft onto them somewhere in their formative years. 'Not looking for an assistant, I suppose?'

'You've got a job.'

'I could moonlight.'

At a guess, he was in his mid-twenties and about the same size and weight I was at his age. His dark hair was held back in a short, tight ponytail and he wore jeans, a long-sleeved navy T-shirt and Doc Martens. I nodded at the object on the chair.

'What's that?'

'Tazer, man.'

'Illegal in this country.'

'So's marijuana and obscene language.'

I laughed and gave him my card. 'You never know, Hank. You never know. I might be able to use you. Where're you from?'

'Where d'you want?'

'Not Texas.'

'I'm not from Texas. Go right in, Mr Hardy.'

Lorraine Master was sitting up against a nest of snowy pillows. Her complexion, which I'd thought of as olive or something close, was several shades lighter. Her features were drawn and I could see lines I hadn't seen before. Her dark eyes, distorted by the anaesthetic, looked all the bigger in her slightly pinched face and she actually looked more attractive, like a rather bigger Edith Piaf. She wore a white hospital gown and she tried to hold her arms out to me. The heavy dressing on her right shoulder stopped the gesture and she winced at the involuntary movement.

'Easy, Lorrie,' I said. 'Jesus, I'm sorry I got you into this.'

Her eyes sparkled through the dulling effect of the painkillers. 'Fuck you, Hardy, you're sexist. Get it right. I got *you* into it.'

18

SHE told me that the police were giving her twenty-four hours to recover from her wound before interviewing her and that O'Connor would be present.

'Mmm.'

'What does that mean?' she said.

'We had a small falling out over the phone. I accused him of helping to set Stewart up.'

'Christ, did he?'

'I don't know. I was trying to pressure him so I could get to see you. It was hard to judge his reaction. Anyway, you've got nothing to worry about.'

'Thanks. I suppose you've been shot lots of times.'

'I'm sorry, I meant—'

She reached for my hand with her left and held it. 'I know what you mean. I don't have any problem with the police. Tell me what you told them and I'll tell them the same.'

'Don't—'

'I'm not stupid, Cliff. I won't make it word for word.'

Her hand was cool and smooth and I was glad to be holding it. 'I'm having trouble saying the right thing. I know you're not stupid, Lorrie. I'm overprotective, I guess.'

'No you're not. You saved my life. I'd say you're exactly protective enough.'

We sat in silence there for a few minutes then we both started talking. We agreed that it all happened too quickly for us to be scared or to record more than fleeting impressions of the gunman. Our impressions matched: medium height and build, dark clothes, decisive action coming in and going out.

She wasn't sentimental about Fay Lewis and Montefiore. She hadn't known them and hadn't liked what she saw of them. 'Would he know that Fay hadn't told us anything?'

I shrugged. 'Dunno. Could he have heard from outside? Was the window by the door open?'

'I heard him.'

'That's right. So maybe he knows Fay didn't say his name. You can probably hear your own name better than any other sound.'

'Does that mean we're safe? Why the guard then?'

'Hank? Don't you like him?'

'He's sweet. Answer the question.'

'At a guess, he's tapped my phone. So he knows about you and he's known about me from early on. I don't know how.'

'Yes you do. O'Connor.'

'Mmm.'

'There's that pissy sound again. Should I sack him?'

'No. We have to keep tabs on all the players. You have to tell him to get me another session with Stewart.'

Our hands separated and she said, 'Oh?'

'I'm betting this bit of business will have had an effect on him. I've got the tape of our voices and the door breaking and the shots.'

She lay back on the pillows and a wave of fatigue and worry seemed to wash over her. 'I'm tired, Cliff. Could you make sure that Britt's got the children safe and okay? She can bring them in later and hire some more help. As for what you're saying about Stewart, I wouldn't be too sure.'

Hank was still looking alert and ready for action. I asked him to ring O'Connor on his mobile. He did and handed the phone to me.

'Who's this?'

'Hardy,' I said.

'Christ, what now?'

'I want to see Master again. Set it up as quick as you can.'

'You should be in there with him. Maybe you will be. How is she?'

'Good that you got around to asking. She's pretty knocked about and concerned for her kids, but she's not quitting.'

'I've been thinking about that outrageous allegation you made. It's nonsense, but I assume you've uncovered something that bears on Master's situation?'

'Something, not enough. I'm hoping for more.'

'From Stewart?'

'Perhaps. Perhaps from others.'

'We should have a talk if you've got some solid information. I don't much like what's happening—people getting shot.'

'Not when one of those people could be you.'

I heard his exasperated sigh. 'You're determined to be . . . recalcitrant. I'll make the arrangements for you to see Master and leave a message. I'm going to be there when the police talk to Lorraine tomorrow. I hope you're not.'

'No way, I'll be knuckle dragging down some mean street.'

'You're impossible.' He hung up. He was getting good at that.

I handed the phone back to Hank. 'Thanks.'

'Okay. Trouble with the lawyer?'

'No more than usual. D'you get relieved sometime?'

'Sure.' He looked at his watch. 'In an hour.'

'Got a car here?'

'I do.'

'How are you at debugging?'

He practically hugged me. 'I'm the best and I've got the latest stuff.'

'I suppose you're a computer hotshot as well.'

'Mac, PC, networks, I'm there.'

'Hank,' I said, 'this could be the beginning of a beautiful friendship.'

He laughed. 'Bogie.'

I was relieved that he got the reference. 'There's a wine bar down the street. Meet me there when you're free and we'll do some business.'

Hank drove a Nissan Patrol 4WD and lived in Dover Heights. We called by his flat while he explained to his girlfriend, Pammy, an intense, bespectacled young woman, that he was moonlighting for me. She wasn't pleased. I said it was only for a few hours but she still wasn't pleased. Hank loaded some of those metal boxes into the Patrol and we were off.

'Pammy's not happy,' I said.

'Pammy doesn't do happy. She'll be okay.'

We went to my office and I could see that Hank loved everything about it—the décor, the smell, Stephanie Geller next door. I didn't have the heart to tell him about the rent and the plumbing. He went straight to work with his gadgets and in no time flat located listening and monitoring devices in my telephone and fax.

'You've been penetrated, man,' he said.

'Thanks. Just leave them be, okay?'

'You sure? I can—'

'Have a look at the computer.'

I showed him the message with the hotmail address. The Power Mac isn't new and he almost curled his lip, but he settled down in front of it and started in with those rapid action things computer experts do that make my head spin. He inserted a compact disc and stared at me.

'What?'

'Give me your password.'

I told him and his fingers flicked over the keys. He looked annoyed at the time menus took to come up and be eliminated but he persisted. I made mugs of instant coffee and by the time I got back he was tapping his fingers on the desk. He looked at the mug.

'What's this?'

'Instant coffee.'

'Jesus. Okay, thanks. It's tricky, excising an address, but it can be done and it can be traced. That's the good news.'

'Give me the bad news.'

'My kind of guy. This came from an Internet café in the city. Sender was good, knew what to do. Have you ever used those things?'

'Once or twice.'

'You know how it works. You give your name, Hank, and pay in cash.'

I drank the coffee and Hank didn't. He played around some more but he couldn't have found out anything I wouldn't have wanted him to know. I haven't had the computer long enough to put many case files on it and from what I'd seen I was beginning to think I wouldn't in future. There still seemed to be something to say for folders and a strong, locked filing cabinet, maybe with a noxious anti-theft device.

We picked up a pizza and some beer and went to my house where Hank repeated the debugging procedure with similar results. Like any good young entrepreneur he had his own company and was under contract to the security firm O'Connor had employed. He said he'd send me an invoice online.

'You'll get a cheque in the mail.'

'You can pay me online.'

I looked at him as I opened the pizza and handed him a beer.

'Okay, okay,' he said, ' a cheque it is. But you should move with the times, Cliff.'

We were sitting at the breakfast bench in my kitchen. I waved a slice of pizza at him. 'I have, and look where it's got me. Any arsehole who wants to can know my business. I suppose my mobile's insecure as well.'

He chewed, drank and swallowed, then used one of the paper napkins that came with the pizza. Good manners. 'Unlikely, and you need some pretty high-tech equipment to intercept cell phone calls, especially if it's digital. Where is it?'

'It is digital and it's in my car at the garage. The NRMA had to tow it for me after the tyres got slashed.'

He was about to take another bite but he stopped and his jaw fell. 'No shit? What's this all about? Hey, dumb question. You can't tell me.'

'No. Sorry, it's complicated and I don't really know what it's all about myself.'

I used his mobile to leave messages for O'Connor and Lorrie via the guard at the hospital that my office and home phones were insecure and my mobile not available, then we sat and ate and drank for a while. He knew when to keep quiet and when to talk. He inspected my CD, vinyl and cassette collection without throwing up and took an intelligent interest in the books. I was glad of his company and an idea was forming in my mind. We tidied away the remains of the meal and the cans and I put a pot of real coffee on to perc.

'Are you working tomorrow?'

He nodded. 'Evening shift. Free in the day.'

'How're you in boats?' I said.

It was barely light the next morning when Hank and I lowered the aluminium dinghy I'd borrowed from Clive, my fishing fanatic neighbour, into the water at Birchgrove after making sure Penny's yacht was still where it had been. We'd transported the dinghy on the top of Hank's Patrol and the only thing that dampened his enthusiasm was the set of oars.

'I can get us an outboard, Cliff.'

'So could I. I want to be quiet. Element of surprise.'

'I've got the tazer. You reckon that shooter's going to be there?'

'Do you think I'd go unarmed and take you along if I did?'

'I guess not.'

'Right. No, I suppose you could say I'm just fishing.'

I was wearing jeans and sneakers and they got wet, as I expected, but we got underway and I pointed out the direction. Hank's strong oar strokes were irregular but better than mine. The few times I've tried to row I've sent the boat in circles. The harbour water was smooth and we made good time. The *You Beaut* was bobbing gently at its mooring.

'Nice boat,' Hank said.

'The owner says it's a yacht.'

'Whatever. You've been on it?'

'In Noumea.'

'Wow. Okay, we come alongside and then what?'

I pointed. 'We go up that ladder, if that's what they call it.'

Hank brought the dinghy to where the ladder reached down almost to the water level and I tied it to the bottom rung. The dinghy bumped against the yacht a few times before it settled into place and I wondered how the sound would carry. We waited a few seconds but no reaction came from above so we went up onto the deck, me first. Hank had the stun gun on his belt and I gestured for him to keep it there.

Up close, the yacht showed signs of wear and tear. The spick and span appearance I'd noticed at Noumea was long gone. The woodwork was salt spattered and the metal fittings were dull. There were seagull droppings in various places and the sails lashed to the masts were stained and tired-looking. I moved forward towards the hatch. The yacht rocked a little, reacting to a slight wake from some other boat. I reached for the handrail and snatched my hand away.

Hank saw it at the same time as me. The handrail was smeared for a couple of metres with something brown and sticky. A couple of flies had been caught in it as it dried and others were buzzing around it now.

'Don't touch anything,' I said.

The hatch was open and I went down the steps keeping my hands to my sides.

It's always the same—you can hear it and smell it before you see it. The flies buzzed like mini chainsaws and the blood gave off that stink that comes when it meets the air and dries. Add in the emptied bowels. Reg Penny lay on the floor of the saloon where we'd had our uneasy conversation those few weeks ago. No neat kill this. He'd been stabbed several times and the blood had flowed until one of the stabs hit his heart. He was bare-chested, the only way I'd ever seen him, and the wounds were dark on his tanned skin, with dried blood over his torso where the flies were taking off and landing and fighting over the spoils.

Blood was spattered over a fair distance, presumably from when the knife had been thrust home, retracted and thrust again, and again. The floor of the saloon between the body and the door wasn't bloodied, which was why there were no footprints, but blood-smeared fingers had clutched the rail beside the hatch steps and beyond. I tried to block Hank but he leaned over me and got a full view of the scene.

'Jee-zus!'

'Don't throw up. The SOC guys don't like bagging it.'

'Who is he?'

'Was. The bloke we came to see.'

'What do we do?'

I was feeling shaky. This had been a vigorous man, considerably younger than me, dabbling in dangerous matters but alive just twenty-four hours ago and probably for longer than that. I recalled the careless way he'd tossed the beer bottle into the water and sauntered away with his young companion. A moment frozen in time for me and caught on my camera. The weirdness of it made me short-tempered.

'What do you think? What would they tell you in the TAFE course. To split?'

'I don't know.'

'Of course you don't.' I sucked in a breath and almost gagged myself. Some mentor. 'Sorry, Hank,' I said. 'This is my third body in two days. It's getting to me. What you do is you go back up on deck, get in a few breaths of fresh air, and call the police.'

'You?'

'Don't worry about it.'

19

THE saloon-cum-kitchen wasn't hard to search, because there was very little in it and what there was Penny had arranged pretty neatly—the books and magazines, technical manuals about the yacht's equipment, eating and cooking utensils, maps and charts, tools, playing cards, board games. I picked through it as quickly as I could, disturbing it as little as possible. I was looking for anything that might give me a lead on the Noumea mystery man and/or the young man I'd seen on the yacht the day before. Nothing there.

The sleeping quarters consisted of two bunks, three-quarter bed size. The top bunk was unmade with just a mattress and a pillow. The bottom bunk had two pillows and sheets with a light duvet bunched up near the foot. The bunk had been slept in and, at a guess, fucked in. There were stains and traces of cigarette ash. A bottle of massage oil stood on the floor near the bunk along with a box of tissues, personal lubricant and a packet of condoms. It looked as if Penny had practised safe sex, or thought he had.

His clothes hung in a shallow closet and were stacked, neatly again, in a set of drawers. Jackets, trousers, shirts, T-shirts, shorts, jeans, boxers, Y-fronts, socks. Nothing out of the ordinary. I was looking for a diary, a journal, the log, a notebook, anywhere information might be recorded. There was no Rolodex, no laptop. Either Penny was remarkably free of the impulse to record information, names and events, or his killer had got there first. In a folder lying on the top bunk, buff-coloured like the mattress so that I didn't spot it at first, was a sheaf of financial records relating to the yacht. I leafed through them, but they appeared to be specific and unin-teresting, although there were invoices for parts and labour from a ship's engineer in Noumea, dated the day I'd given Penny the money.

Time was running short. No passport, which certainly suggested an earlier search and removal exercise. Penny's tobacco packet lay beside the pillow and I moved it to look under the pillow. It felt more solid than it should have. I opened it and found a miniature audio cassette, nestled in with the tobacco and the papers.

Hank's voice came from above. 'Cliff, the cops are here.'

I stuffed the cassette down inside my left sock and went through the saloon, past the body and back up into the begin-ning of the day.

I got Hammond and Carmichael again, and they were even less happy than the day before. College Street again.

'You didn't tell us anything about this boat,' Carmichael said with the tape running. 'Why not?'

'You didn't ask.'

'How could we? What were you looking for out there—the guy who shot at you?'

'Yeah. That's why I didn't have a gun and took the kid.'

'Why did you take him?' Hammond looked concerned.

'To row the boat. I'm no oarsman.'

Carmichael said, 'He was carrying a stun gun. They're illegal.'

I shrugged. 'That's what I told him, but he works in security. They probably all carry them, I wouldn't know.'

And so it went on. I told them all I knew about Penny and his connection with Montefiore and Fay Lewis and Stewart Master. I told them that I'd seen the boat at Balmain the day before. I didn't tell them about the young man aboard, or the photographs I'd taken or about the cassette that was creating a blister on my foot inside my sock.

They were sceptical, experienced interrogators, but this time around they got no more out of me than I'd wanted to give.

'We'll be keeping an eye on you, Hardy,' Carmichael said when the tape had been turned off.

'Good,' I said. 'With the balaclava boy around I can use the protection. What about Bachelor?'

'He'll be charged with possession of an illegal instrument.'

'Great. That could screw up his career nicely.'

'Tough,' Carmichael said. 'I hope your public liability policy's paid up, Hardy. That Yank could sue you for everything you've got for getting him in this shit. You know the way they are. In fact, I just might give him the idea.'

'You disappoint me, Inspector. I thought the police service was trying for better relations with the citizenry.'

Hammond looked embarrassed as she wound the tape back, but Carmichael wasn't fazed. 'That doesn't include a cowboy nuisance like you.'

I'd had enough of him. 'Fuck you, Carmichael. That kid conducted himself well. He didn't freak when he saw the mess; he kept your crime scene clean and he called in straight off the way I told him to. If you heavy him he's likely to turn into just another cowboy nuisance like me. That's how we're made.'

Carmichael let go one of his patent sneers. 'Is that so? Well, I'll have to look into the chances of deporting him.'

Great work, Cliff, I thought. I walked out of the College Street station into the mid-morning. Hank Bachelor was nowhere around; Lorrie Master was in hospital and I'd possibly buggered up Bachelor's job prospects. I was at a low ebb, but at least I'd had the sense not to retrieve the cassette from my sock until I was safely inside the cab taking me to Drummoyne, to the NRMA approved garage where I collected my car and paid for four new tyres. They were probably overdue.

It was well on into the afternoon when I got to Glebe and the moment I stepped out of the car I heard a yell.

'Hey, Cliff, what about my tinny?'

'Jesus, Clive, I forgot all about it. I had some trouble with the cops and it's tied up at the Balmain wharf.'

'I hope the buggers haven't impounded it.'

'No, it'll be right. I'll get the young bloke onto it.'

Clive said okay and I made a mental note to get him a slab. That reminded me, I'd eaten nothing since before dawn. I microwaved a few slices of the leftover pizza and opened a Hahn light. That all went down well so I heated up some of the previous night's coffee and took it into the sitting room with the cassette and my recorder. I was about to press 'Play' when the thought occurred to me that the room itself might be bugged as well as the phone.

I regrouped in the back yard. It's about five metres by five, bricked with weeds poking through, and some native plants around the edges struggling against persistent neglect. I brushed leaves and unidentifiable pollution from one of the two deck chairs and was set to go when the mobile, which I'd also brought out to complete the set-up, rang.

'Hardy.'

'Hey, Cliff, this is Hank, Hank Bachelor.'

My heart would have sunk except that he sounded so happy. 'You're the only Hank I know, Hank, so there's no need for the surname. I was all ready to apologise but you sound uppish.'

'Man, am I up? I've just had the greatest experience. With the cops and all? The report I can put on to my teacher on policing, surveillance, interview technique? Man, I've got it made.'

'What about the charge for carrying an illegal—?'

'Instrument? That's a blast. The security company's been dying for a test case on the law. They couldn't be happier.'

'I'm not sure I want one of my investigations to become a high-profile test case, Hank.'

'It's months away, Cliff. Months away. We'll have this thing unscrambled by then.'

'We?'

'Sure. Here's my mobile number.' He recited it and I wrote it down in the notebook I'd had ready to make notes on the tape. 'I'll be watchin' over your lady again tonight.'

I asked him if he could recover the dinghy and deliver it back to Clive and he said he would.

'Right, Hank. Thanks.'

'Thank *you*! We'll stay in touch, won't we, Cliff?'

He rang off. I put the phone down slowly. Was there some sort of threat, an implied pressure, in his last remark? No, not Hank. Surely not.

I set the recorder on a brick and hit 'Play'. There were some indeterminate sounds before a voice spoke clearly.

Montefiore: 'I'm getting so fuckin' sick of this. How long does he say now?'

Lewis: 'You heard him. Stop whingeing. A couple of days.'

Montefiore: 'I could do with a drink and a fuck.'

Lewis: 'Yeah, that'd be right. In that order.'

Montefiore: 'I didn't mean it like that.'

Lewis: 'Just go to sleep.'

Montefiore: 'C'mon, Fay.'

Lewis: 'No, he'll hear us. Anyhow, you should complain. I'm out of smokes and nicotine's more addictive than alcohol . . . and heroin.'

Montefiore: 'Yeah, yeah. You can smoke yourself to death when we get the money. Shit, sorry, love. Didn't mean that. This fuckin' boat . . .'

Lewis: 'Is it any wonder I won't tell you the name? How could I trust you?'

Montefiore: 'I could make you tell me.'

Lewis: 'No, you wouldn't have the guts.'

Montefiore: 'You're right, torturing women's not my scene. Anyway, I *know* the name, so really you're just along for the fuckin' ride, aren't you?'

Lewis: 'You don't know it.'

Montefiore: 'Eastman, right? Frank Eastman. That's when he wasn't Phil West.'

Lewis: 'Wrong.'

Montefiore: 'I don't think so. I talked to Rory, remember, before he went missing and you fucked that bastard?'

Lewis: 'Jesus, Jay. Let it rest.'

Montefiore: 'I'm getting most of that dough back from Reg.'

Lewis: 'You're all talk.'

Montefiore: 'No, listen, I know this gay guy in Sydney. Just Reg's type, looks ten years younger than he is. I'll line him up with Reg and he'll find the money and—'

Lewis: 'Talk, talk, talk . . .'

There was more—squabbling, bitching, contradicting each other, both on edge from withdrawal and tension. Eventually they went to sleep just before the tape ran out. I tried the reverse side but it was blank. I rewound the tape and played it again without learning anything more.

A number of questions arose. Had Penny played the tape? Probably, although I hadn't seen a recorder in my quick search. Perhaps he'd set the recorder up with a fresh tape to record more of the intimacies between his passengers. In that case the police were likely to find it and God knows what could be on it. If Penny had heard the tape, it was unlikely he would have allowed Montefiore to provide him with a playmate, however attractive. So the man I'd seen on the boat probably wasn't Montefiore's acquaintance. Was he Penny's killer or had the Noumea mystery man done the wet work with a different MO? And where was the Noumea money, whoever had it? If it was on the boat or in the flat the cops would be back to me with more questions. Or playing a waiting game.

I drained the coffee mug and realised that the afternoon had drawn in and was getting cool. My shoulder was aching and I took everything back inside and swallowed some painkillers with a weak scotch and water. I wasn't happy. I was in illicit possession of evidence relating to three homicides; I'd involved two innocent people in dangerous situations, and my relationship with my client had been through some choppy waters and could go there again.

I wandered around the house, thinking, until I heard noises from the front. I looked out and saw Hank Bachelor and Clive lift the aluminium dinghy from the Patrol's roof rack and carry it into Clive's front yard. Hank waved at Clive and drove away.

I heard the chirp of my mobile and went back to the kitchen where I'd left it beside the coffee mug and the dirty plate.

'Hardy.'

'Bryce O'Connor. I've been hearing things about your comings and goings, Hardy. I hope you're not going to need legal representation.'

'So do I.'

'Stewart Master will see you tomorrow at 10 am. I haven't quite put that accurately. In fact, he *insists* on seeing you.'

20

MASTER wasn't the same man. He stalked across to the cubicle ignoring everything else until he was a metre from me, almost within punching distance, and he looked as if there was nothing he'd rather do than land one.

'You cunt,' he said.

'Sorry you feel that way. You don't think you're possibly a bit to blame yourself?'

He dropped into the chair across the table and some of the steam went out of him. 'Yeah, in a way of course it's all my fucking fault, but what sort of an idiot takes a woman into a set-up like that?'

'She was looking at paying out a hell of a lot of money. I thought she should get a look at who she was paying it to and she could bail out if she didn't want to go the whole distance. Also, I thought she was probably a good judge of character, with an exception in your case.'

His eyes narrowed. 'Fuck you. That should go for you as well. So you reckon she's a good judge of character, do you? Been having little chats?'

'Listen, Stewart, I don't give a shit about you. In my book she'd be better to let you rot here for ten years and let your kids grow up without you. Better for them, better for everyone. But I know there's some conspiracy here and you're in the middle of it. Your wife and I have been shot at. Three of the blokes you had dealings with in Noumea are dead and—'

'Three? Rory and Jay, who else?'

'Reg Penny. I found him on his boat yesterday morning with four, let's make that five, knife wounds in his chest. He'd been there a while. It didn't smell good and it didn't look pretty.'

It rocked him. He leaned back in his chair and had trouble stopping himself from covering his face with his hands. Then he surprised me. 'You've seen Lorrie,' he said quietly. 'How is she?'

I'd thought he was the type to worry only about himself and he'd proved me wrong. It gave him points on my scorecard—not a lot, but some. 'She's all right, worried about the kids but that's all in hand. She's got a guard and there'll be one when she goes home. She didn't need major surgery or anything. I imagine she'll have a scar of some kind, but . . .'

He nodded. 'How come you didn't get hit?'

'I pulled Lorrie down. He was mainly concerned to get Fay and Jay. By the time he got to us I'd grabbed a gun that was there and got off a couple of shots. Didn't hit him but he took off.'

He gave me a long, searching look. Had he picked up on my inadvertent use of 'Lorrie'? Hard to tell, but it seemed like the time to put the question. '*Who* is he, Master? What's it all about? Who's Eastman, or is it West?'

He sighed and leaned back in the chair. As before, there were other prisoners and their visitors in the room, but neither of us registered them or the guard. We were both closely focused. I waited while he seemed to turn things over in his mind, weigh them, decide. But he wasn't quite ready. 'Tell me what you know first.'

I gave him Montefiore's version more or less verbatim— that the reward for setting Master up was the green light for a major dope shipment into Australia and a share of the profits. I said that Rory McCloud had knocked it back and been eliminated and that Pascal Rivages was a main player.

'And did you believe all that?'

'I didn't know what to believe. I thought there was something in it, but I couldn't see the point of dropping you in it, or why the prosecutor and the other people at this end would go along, or why *you* appear to have gone along with it.'

'No?'

'I guessed there was something in it when I learned you'd put in a bid for the Atlas. You were looking to make big money somehow.'

He grimaced. 'And you told Lorrie that and she read me the riot act.'

I shrugged. 'I was trying to shake something up.'

'You fucking did.'

'It's my job.'

'Yeah. Everything's changed now. Did he know the woman with you was Lorrie?'

'I hate to say it but I think he could've. I found out later my phones were tapped. I was slack.'

'You were. All right, I'm going to have to trust you, and that goes against the grain. If this goes any further, I'm dead in here. I've asked around. A few blokes say you're a complete prick but you've got some balls and you're not a talker. This is how it was. I was approached to be an inside man in the prison system to track how the drugs were getting in. I was supposed to be convicted of a medium level import, get five years, be out in under three. They were going to move me around and I'd report to them how the system worked. The conviction was going to be overturned and I'd be paid a big compensation with a lot more under the counter.'

'Jesus,' I said. 'Why'd you agree to that?'

'A couple of reasons. One, they were going to do me for a fraud thing and put me inside for a stretch anyway if I didn't play. Two, I couldn't stand being second fiddle to Lorrie. Running that gym was something straight I could do and enjoy and make money at.'

'So what happened?'

'They double-crossed me or fucking triple or quadruple. First, my contact, Eastman or West or whoever the fuck he is, wasn't a federal cop at all. He had been, but now he was a go-between for federal and state cops and some prison officers looking to make a pile. They'd set up the customs blokes and the trial people and that. Two, they planted a shit-load on me and I got what I got. Three, forget about dope. This is about heroin.'

He paused, as if revealing all this that he'd kept secret had taken his breath away. Heroin made sense. Big money. Three dead people—small price to pay.

Master smiled and there was a variety of different emotions in the smile—guilt, shame, anger, even amusement. 'Here's number four and it's the clincher. I'm going to be the way in for the smack. It's all arranged. If I don't do it I serve the ten, probably more. Extensions are easy to arrange.'

'It doesn't sound like such a booming market.'

'You don't understand. Get a lot of these kids hooked, blokes in for short stretches, Abos and Viets especially, and then when you've got them on the outside you've got a

market and people to exploit. All sorts of things an addict'll
do for you if you've got what he wants. How does that grab
you, Hardy?'

A jackhammer started somewhere close by and its clatter
was unnerving. It was my turn to sit back and think. The
visiting time was coming to an end. Everyone's heard of deals
like this, usually when they go wrong, and Master's had gone
wrong in the worst way. He seemed almost to enjoy it except
that his capacity for enjoyment had pretty much left him.

'You haven't answered my question,' he said.

'It wasn't really a question.'

He shook his head. 'No. It's a fuck-up.'

'Right. I'd have to say it's one of the biggest fuck-ups I've
come across.'

His lean features hardened; he didn't look so youthful
and there was a pent-up force in the way he shifted slightly
in his seat. 'You haven't just come across it, Hardy. You're
fucking involved.'

'Time's up.' The guard advanced towards us.

'Stay in touch through O'Connor,' Master said as he
acknowledged the call.

'You trust him?'

He laughed as if what I'd said was the funniest thing he'd
heard all week.

Jumpy wasn't the word for the way I felt as I collected my
stuff from the locker. Master had said the drugs operation
had required the cooperation of people inside the prison
system as it always has. Was someone at Avonlea aware of my
visit? Watching me now? On his mobile to someone outside?
It didn't make for steady hands and good driving. It made

for high-alert tension, keyed-up responses, adrenaline-fuelled reactions and increased perspiration levels. I worked my way back to the main road by a circuitous route. Anyone following me would have stuck out like a frisbee on a golf green.

To clear my head I played a country music station for the first few kilometres back to the city. Robert Johnson's thin but resonant vocals and guitar ripped in. Thanks to a couple of visits to the Blues 'n' Roots festival at Byron Bay where Tess Hewitt, a former girlfriend, lived, I knew a bit about Johnson, the 'king of the Delta blues'. I was reminded of a line about him in the film *Ghosts of Mississippi*—'If I was goin' to sell my soul to the Devil I'd want a lot more than some guitar lessons.' Stewart Master had done something like that and the deal was turning very sour on him. Robert Johnson hadn't lived very long after the supposed deal to exchange his soul for the ability to play delta blues better than anyone ever had.

As things stood, Stewart Master wasn't looking at a long and happy life either. According to his own assessment, if he didn't go along with the arrangement he was dead. If he did, what guarantee did he have that the result wouldn't be much the same? Master, in my revised estimate of him, struck me as tough, possibly fatalistic. There was a chance he'd tell the manipulators to go to hell and take the consequences. Unless extra pressure could be brought to bear on him. That hit me the way the smelling salts do when the trainer puts them under your nose between rounds and tells you what you have to do when you're out there again.

The power of that thought had blotted out Robert Johnson and the phoney stuff that had followed—Waylon Jennings, Garth Brooks. I held the old, wavering car steady in the middle lane with one hand on the wheel as I jabbed at the buttons on my mobile.

'Mrs Master has left the hospital, Mr Hardy.'

'What?' The car swerved as I shouted into the phone. 'What d'you mean she's left?'

'I'm not prepared to be shouted at over the telephone.'

I fought for control. 'I'm sorry. I visited her the other day. I'm helping her with a certain matter. Please tell me what happened.'

The hospital official told me that the police had interviewed Lorrie in the morning and that she had seemed undisturbed by their visit. The doctor had said her progress was satisfactory and she had walked about a little with her arm in a sling. A bit later she had called a person from her office who had brought in some clothes. She'd dressed and checked out of the hospital, signing a waiver form releasing the hospital from any responsibility for her condition and paying her bill in full.

'This person. A young Asian woman?'

'Yes. We're very worried, Mr Hardy. What is happening?'

'I'm not sure. Did she leave with the Asian woman?'

'I'm not sure.'

'I'm on my way to the hospital now. Could you please check on that and see if there's anyone who actually saw her leave.'

'This is very alarming.'

I tried for a non-alarming tone. 'I think there's an explanation but I'd just like to get things straight. Please do as I ask.'

Then I rang Fiona at the office who confirmed that Lorrie had asked her to buy her some clothes and bring them in.

'Buy? Not get from home?'

'No. She was very clear about that, so I did it. I bought her underwear, a blouse and a skirt. She said she had shoes and a jacket. I took them in and she told me to go back to work, so I did. Is there something wrong?'

I smoothed her down as well, and made two more calls, breaking the law by talking as I drove. One was to the Double Bay house where Britt reported that all was well with both children safely home from school and the guard O'Connor had hired in place. Britt sounded shaky, as if being an au pair in Australia suddenly wasn't the safest job in the world as it would've been a short while back. Couldn't blame her.

My next call was to O'Connor, who wasn't available. I left a message for him to contact me on my mobile and to be ready to meet me wherever and whenever I said. The person who took the message made me repeat it three times before he could believe what he was hearing.

At the hospital I was shown straight to the administrator's office. She had another woman with her, a nurse.

'Mr Hardy, I'm Felicity Warwick and this is Nurse Havel. I'm very concerned about your telephone call and its implications.'

'I don't think it's anything for the hospital to worry about at this stage,' I said. 'I understand Mrs Master received a telephone call today.'

The administrator checked a sheet. 'In fact she made two calls. One to a taxi company, although we would have happily done that for her.'

'And the other?'

'Yes, before the call to the taxi.'

I recited my mobile number and she nodded. 'I wouldn't have told you of course, but since you appear to know . . .'

I'd left the mobile in the locker at Avonlea where it could ring till its batteries died. The sinking feeling I'd had since

I'd phoned the hospital got deeper but I tried not to show too much alarm. Like all bureaucrats, she didn't want any problems and any she had she wanted to go away. The bullet wound, the guard, the police and me all spelled trouble she didn't need. It wasn't hard to jolly her along.

'Thanks for your cooperation, Ms Warwick. I—'

'Mrs.' She smiled. She could see relief in sight.

'Mrs Warwick. I'm sure things can be sorted out. I take it Nurse Havel here saw Mrs Master leave?'

The young nurse almost bobbed her head as Mrs Warwick indicated that she could speak.

'Yes, sir. I saw the lady leave.'

'In a taxi?'

'No, sir. She waits, the taxi comes and then another car. She gives money to the taxi man and then she leaves in the other car.'

'What kind of car?'

'Sir?'

'Can you describe the car?'

'Big,' she said.

I was in my office when O'Connor's call came through. I was staring at the computer screen, which was something I was likely to do more and more as time went on. It made me wonder how much longer I wanted to do this kind of work.

'Hardy, what the devil are you playing at leaving a message like that? If you're trying to humiliate me it's been tried by experts.'

'No. Hard though it might be for you to believe, I wasn't thinking about you at all. Not really.'

'Are you drunk? I take it this is about your meeting with the wretched Master?'

'I'm not drunk, although I'm thinking about it. This isn't about Stewart, it's about Lorraine. Let me read you what's on my computer screen.

' "Hardy, stay out of this or she's dead." '

21

BRYCE O'Connor looked around my office as if he was thinking he wouldn't park his golf cart in a place like this. In fact I'd cleaned it up a bit while I was waiting for him, more to give myself something to do while I was thinking than out of professional pride. Eventually he sank into the uncomfortable client's chair and was so agitated he didn't notice the discomfort.

'Tell me,' he said.

I gave him what I had, referring to my notes, producing the photographs, printouts of the emails, everything. He was in his business suit, but somehow his grooming seemed to have slipped a little. I'd have thought a criminal lawyer would be fairly used to the seamy side but maybe he'd always tried to keep himself aloof, and aloof wasn't really an option now.

'We have to go to the police with this,' he said when I'd finished.

'Perhaps I haven't made myself clear. The police, some police, are involved in this up to their necks. So are some lawyers, some customs people, possibly some politicians.'

'So what do you suggest?'

'I've been thinking it through. All I've been trying to do is to make up some ground for Master, because that's what Lorrie wanted even if he didn't.'

'I understand that. My object has been the same.'

'So you say. Maybe I believe you.'

'I resent that.'

'Resent away. For the moment, I'm going to trust you.'

He was younger than me, better educated, much richer and with far better prospects, but he knew that he was out of his depth this time. His natural inclination, a well-worn groove, would be to patronise a sub-professional like me and refuse to be talked down to, but he knew he had to take it.

'Go on,' he said.

'My object's changed. Now I'm worried about Lorrie and her alone. Master's just an incidental as far as I'm concerned.'

'I don't follow.'

'You're the avenue to him. What you have to do is tell him about this. Tell him his children have been threatened and his wife's been kidnapped and—'

'You didn't say anything about the children.'

'Think about it. How else do you reckon they got her out of the hospital, got her to fake a call for a taxi and got her into a waiting car?'

'I see what you mean.'

'You have to talk to Master. He must know more about this Eastman or West or whoever he is. He has to tell us how to get a line on him.'

He nodded eagerly. 'Then the police?'

'Maybe, depending on the quality of the information. In a strange way this latest development works in our favour.'

He looked at me as if I'd suddenly started speaking in Esperanto. 'How on earth do you arrive at that conclusion?'

'My guess is that by taking Lorrie, this bastard who's doing all this shit thinks he's gained a greater measure of control over Master and me. I think he's wrong as far as Master's concerned, at least. I think he's broken cover.'

He agreed to talk to Master and report back as soon as possible. I stressed that it had to be in person, that I didn't trust any of the usual means of communication. I also told him to make reassuring arrangements at Lorrie's place of business and at the house.

'Like what?'

'Like whatever your high-priced brain can think up. You've made a lot of money out of the Masters, and now you're going to earn it.'

He protested. 'I'm a busy man.'

'Make time. If this setting up of Master comes out, it doesn't look good for you either way.'

He was a few steps from the door but he stopped. 'What do you mean?'

'If you were part of it you're going to stink; if you weren't, you're going to look foolish.'

He considered that. 'And you have the say?'

'We'll see.'

I was on thin ice and I knew it. I didn't really think that O'Connor was involved at the dirty end, or anywhere along the line, but it suited me to keep him on his toes. The more agitated he was, the more it should communicate to Master and I wanted him to be *very* edgy, at least as edgy as me. I had a sense that Eastman/West was under pressure and that he was operating alone. He seemed to be a hands-on type and they don't like delegating and trusting others. Snatching

Lorrie, I judged, was out of character. He tended to clean the decks immediately he was threatened. Where the present pressure was coming from I could only guess. Maybe the shipment had arrived. Maybe his various masters were getting alarmed at the body count. Perhaps his judgement was faltering. Good. But all that meant was that mine had to be spot-on.

One thing was for sure, I wasn't going into this on my own. I needed allies. Still using the mobile, much as I disliked it, I phoned Frank Parker and arranged to see him later that night.

Frank and his wife Hilde, a former tenant of mine, live in Bronte in a modest semi with a view of the water, meaning it's worth a hell of a lot more money than they paid for it. Their son Peter, my anti-godson, drops in now and then when he can spare time from his travels for Greenpeace. Frank met me at the door and shook my hand; Hilde hugged me; Peter wasn't there.

'I think he's in Nepal,' Hilde said, 'doing something with the Fred Hollows Foundation.'

'Vietnam,' Frank said, pouring scotch.

Hilde shrugged. 'Who knows? You look stressed, Cliff.'

'He always looks stressed except when he's pissed,' Frank said. 'It's the only way he knows how to look.'

'More stressed then.'

Frank nodded. 'Yeah. What is it, Cliff? How can I help?'

Frank has no secrets from Hilde. I envy their relationship which seems to be based on affection, shared experience and something else. I've had the first two in my time, but I've missed out on the something else. Just being with them has a calming effect on me, and I was able to tell them the story fully and reasonably coherently, only backing up a few times to fill in things when they asked questions.

'Jesus, Cliff,' Frank said when I finished. 'That's a sticky one, even for you.'

'I know.'

Hilde shook her head and went off to make coffee. I hadn't eaten since breakfast and she could see that the whisky was getting to me. I could feel it too. But I wanted more and had some. Hilde came back with a coffee pot on a tray with plates of rye bread, sliced ham, cheese and pickles.

'Bit late for that, love,' Frank said.

'I don't think so. Cliff is . . . what's the word? Whacked. But he has to stay awake while you make your calls. He'll have to contribute something probably. Then he can sleep in Peter's room.'

What if Peter breezes in from Nepal or Vietnam? I thought. I was losing it, as Sinatra said on his deathbed, but I knew Hilde was right and I accepted a mug of black coffee after she depressed the plunger. I loaded up a slice of the rye bread. 'You heard her, Frank,' I said. 'I'm sorry to put you through it but . . .'

Frank, in his early sixties but still limber from golf, swimming and love, rose from his chair and poured himself coffee. 'Save me some of those bread and butter cucumbers,' he said.

That was Frank. What I was asking him to do was to call in favours he'd rather not call in and talk to people he'd rather not talk to. There was no point in going to straight shooters in the federal or state police, Frank was going to talk to some of those others—the bagmen, the fixers, the jokers, as they were known. Frank's contacts would be mostly retired by now, some voluntarily, some by mutual agreement. But they stayed in touch with the criminal world they'd paddled in for so long. They had to—there were networks of obligation there as well. They went to each other's funerals, sometimes sporting their Masonic regalia, put condolence notices in the papers, and some genuinely grieved and some breathed sighs of relief.

I sat with Hilde and drank coffee and ate some of the food she'd laid out and we talked about her stints as Third World dental assistant and about Peter, of whom she was very proud.

'I'm sorry to put Frank through this,' I said. 'He'll hate talking to some of those bastards.'

Hilde nodded. 'Yes. But in a way he won't mind too much. He misses it all sometimes. I can tell. I see him going off to golf and I know that it's a substitute for what was his real life.'

'You and Peter are his real life.'

'Yes. I know that and he knows it and that's what makes it all right. Better than that. Good. But I could feel a . . . rise in his foot. No, what am I trying to say?'

After so many years in Australia, Hilde's English is fluent but some things still trip her up.

'A spring in his step,' I said.

'Yes. He is interested. A little bit of this sometimes is better for him than golf and gardening. I hope it's just a little bit.'

'It will be.'

We talked about nothing in particular for a while until Frank came back. He had a pad with some notes on it in his hand. 'I'll have to eat this when we're finished. Put it on a piece of bread with ham and pickles.'

'You are a fool,' Hilde said.

Frank settled himself and poured some coffee. He added a touch of whisky and consulted the notes. 'Couldn't get much on Warren North, which is apparently his real name. Shadowy type. With ASIO for a while, then undercover for the feds. The feeling is he went rogue some time back but still represents himself as official when it suits him. Plausible in the part, they say.'

'A killer?'

Frank nodded. 'Rumoured to be. You know what it's like in that game. More veils than Salome.'

'No clues as to where he might go for a bolthole, especially with a hostage?'

'Nothing. But you've got a bit lucky on the other side of the street. It's all a bit vague, but there've been rumours of a shipment of heroin coming in and the usual channels being bypassed. And that's made certain people very unhappy.'

Frank drank his spiked coffee and went quiet. I knew what he was thinking. He hated the bent cops and the semi-bent ones, and especially those who kept their own hands clean while facilitating the dirty work to be done by others. They were paid off, not in money, but in information that allowed them to make certain arrests and claim successes and earn promotions and perks—personal assistants, study tours, legitimate performance increments to their salaries. Frank could probably have gone to the top if he'd played this game but he refused and he hated dealing with those who had played it.

'Okay,' he said. 'The name North rang a bell or two and a couple of people are on the lookout for you. It's going to cost you money.'

'There's money.'

'And it could get messy. If this information's right, North could be regarded as expendable.'

'He's killed three people that I know of. I regard him as a waste of space.'

'Yeah, but you'll have to put some distance between yourself and him when and if the moment comes. You know what I'm saying, Cliff. You've got a few counts against you and there's people keeping score.'

He was referring to my several licence suspensions and my brief stint in Berrima gaol. I tried for a contrite look.

'Here's one of the parts you won't like. You have to have a meeting with Black Andy Piper. I don't even like saying his bloody name.'

22

EX-CHIEF Inspector Andrew Piper, known as Black Andy, was one of the most corrupt cops ever to serve in New South Wales. He'd risen rapidly through the ranks, a star recruit with a silver medal in the modern pentathlon at the Tokyo Olympics. He was big and good-looking and he had all the credentials—a policeman father, the Masonic connection, marriage to the daughter of a middle-ranking state politician, two children, a boy and a girl. Black Andy had played a few games for South Sydney and boxed exhibitions with Tony Mundine. He'd headed up teams of detectives in various Sydney divisions and the crimes they'd solved were only matched by the ones they'd taken the profits from. His name came up adversely at a succession of enquiries and he eventually retired on full benefits because to pursue him hard would have brought down more of the higher echelon of the force than anyone could handle.

I knew that Frank had had several collisions with him and had come off worse each time. I'd run into him once myself when I was trying to help my client face down a protection racket in the Cross. Black Andy and two of his offsiders had discouraged me to the extent of putting me in hospital for a few days. My client paid up and then sold up.

Frank and I sat silent with our memories.

'Piper,' Hilde said. 'I remember him.'

'You should,' Frank said. 'He put the hard word on you the way he did with every good-looking wife of every policeman.'

'He had dyed hair,' Hilde said. 'And cold eyes.'

Frank sipped coffee that had to be cold by now. 'That's him. His hair was as black the day he left as the day he started.'

'Where and when?' I said.

Frank suddenly looked weary, as if bad memories and lost causes had tired him. 'Tomorrow at noon. Greek restaurant opposite the Marrickville RSL.'

'Does he know where . . . North is, or where he might be?'

Frank shrugged. 'The word is that he might, if anyone does. I'd like to go along with you and give him a few kicks to the balls. That's what he did to you, wasn't it?'

'Him and two others.'

'Time to sleep,' Hilde said. 'A kick to the balls never solved anything.'

Peter's room, still bearing some traces of his presence in the form of books on shelves and rock star posters, was strangely comforting. The three-quarter bed had a secure feel to it, unlike my bed, which somehow always feels as if there should be someone in it with me. As I drifted off I wondered if Peter had ever slept here with a girlfriend. Probably, and with Frank and Hilde's blessing. Very different in my day . . . My mind was wandering and I was checking off things that had improved, with painless dentistry at the top of the list.

I slept soundly for a couple of hours and then was wide awake with a mildly buzzing head from the whisky. I dressed and crept around the familiar house in my socks. I drank several glasses of water with three aspirin and sat by the living-room window watching the day come to life. I opened the window and heard the seagulls on the beach and the hum of early morning traffic. I wondered where Lorrie was and what she was seeing and hearing. I knew she was tough, but confinement does strange things to the mind and some people never recover from it.

It had been a mistake to take her to the Balmain meeting. My judgement had been affected by the attraction I'd felt for her. The mistake had made her vulnerable, but North could probably have taken her from wherever she was. I wasn't going to rack myself about that, but I wasn't going to give myself good marks either. Again, I considered O'Connor's role in the scheme of things. Had he been complicit? Had the guard at the hospital backed off too readily? That made me think of Hank Bachelor and his stun gun, probably now in police possession. Like the rest of Jay and Fay's money. I could use some of that money now. I'd told Frank money was available but I hadn't thought it through. Another thing for O'Connor to sort out.

The daylight had won the battle with the dark and the water and aspirin had put the headache to rest. I was thinking about eating when I heard the unmistakable sound of someone else in the house trying to be quiet. Frank came into the room wearing a dark blue nightshirt that reached just below his knees. He stopped when he saw me at the window.

'Looks good on you, Frank,' I said. 'No buttons, no cord to lose.'

'Hilde likes 'em. Peter takes the piss of course. What're you doing up this early?'

'Raking it all over, what else? This could end badly, mate.'

'Coffee?'

I nodded and went back to worrying. When Frank returned he handed me a mug and the warmth and smell of it lifted my mood a fraction.

'One thing I forgot to tell you last night,' Frank said. 'Carmichael and Hammond are okay. You could bring them in.'

'Thanks, Frank. That's good news. Any tips for dealing with Black Andy?'

'I understand he's a lot smoother now, married to a judge and with all those legal connections.'

'Hold on. He was married to some politician's daughter. A fashion designer or something.'

Frank shook his head. 'She finally left. No, he's married to Mary Pappas. She's—what's wrong?'

The name had hit me like a short left hook. When I'd told Frank the story I hadn't given him all the names. 'Frank, tell me about these legal connections.'

'Oh, his daughter from the first marriage, she's married to John L'Estrange, the barrister, and—'

'Jesus Christ. You've just named the judge and the prosecutor at Master's trial. Black Andy must be in this up to his neck.'

'I've never heard that Pappas is . . . flexible, but . . . She's a hardliner, sure, but I don't know about corrupt.'

'She doesn't need to be. It was mounted as a legitimate undercover federal and state operation, except that there was another agenda.'

Frank absorbed that as he stroked his grey bristled chin. 'No wonder Black Andy wanted to talk to you. This puts a different slant on it. If he's in on it with North and the others.'

'What was your impression?'

'It's hard to say with those bastards. Like I said, I thought they were worried about this uncontrolled shipment, but now I'm not sure. Let me think for a minute. I'm hungry. Want something to eat?'

'About four slices of buttered toast.'

'Brain food. Come on.'

We went out to the kitchen and Frank loaded the toaster and topped up the coffee mugs.

'I hope you're thinking,' I said. 'This just about stymies me.'.

The toaster popped and he buttered the toast. 'I recorded the conversations. Let me just play a few of them back and I'll listen to them again with this stuff in mind.'

He went off with his plate and his mug and I sat there and played with the coffee and the toast. I would have liked to listen to the tapes as well, but Frank was running that part of the show and I had to abide by his judgement. He was still a cop, and a cop's instincts are different to anyone else's.

After a few minutes I realised I'd emptied the mug and all the toast was gone and I hadn't tasted any of it. I stretched and went out into the small back yard where the dew on the grass was just beginning to dry out. I did a few knee bends and flexes and worked the shoulder. It was stiff but not too bad.

Frank rapped on the doorframe and I went back inside. I could hear Hilde moving around in another part of the house and the radio playing the classical music she liked to listen to in the morning.

'It's just a feeling,' Frank said. 'But I get the impression someone's pissed off at the way it's gone ballistic.'

'Hope you're right.'

I thanked Frank and promised to stay in touch. He looked worried. I felt worried. The early morning traffic was thick and I had to concentrate on my driving. My clothes felt musty and my unshaven face itched. I hit the horn too often and had some narrow escapes from drivers who were as ill-tempered and impatient as me.

My mobile rang as I turned into my street and I swore as I answered it and shuffled the car into a tight parking spot.

'Hardy.'

'This is Bryce O'Connor. Have you heard the news?'

'What news? How'd you get on with Master?'

'Stewart Master has escaped.'

23

THE car hadn't quite come to a stop and I had to stand on the brake to stop it bumping the one in front. I swore again and O'Connor's voice sputtered in my ear.

'Is that all you can say?'

'Sorry. I was driving. When was this?'

'They don't know. He was missed this morning.'

'Did you talk to him yesterday?'

'Of course I did. I tried to get him to tell me anything he could about this Eastman. He said nothing and he hung up on me. I tried to call back and he refused to take the calls. What the hell am I going to do? The police are coming to talk to me this morning.'

'For God's sake, don't tell them anything about Lorrie. Just be your above-it-all self. Everything between you and your client is confidential, etc.'

'I'm not sure that'll do under the circumstances.'

'It'll have to do. I'm working on this and I've got some help. That's all I can tell you.'

'What if Master contacts *me*?'

'Not likely, but if he does just tell him what I've told you and give him my mobile number. I'll meet him anywhere, any time. But say as little about me as you possibly can to the police.'

'They'll know you visited him and they know you're working for his wife. Oh my God, they'll try to contact her.'

'They won't succeed, will they?'

I rang off and sat in the car thinking about it. I wished I knew more about Warren North—how he thought, how long his fuse was, how he'd react to this news. Was it good or bad for Lorrie? Would Master know where North was likely to take her? And would he intervene on his own and, if so, with what resources? How would this affect Piper and the people he was associated with? Lots of questions, no answers, as usual.

I went inside, stripped off, showered and shaved, and put on fresh clothes. The light on the answering machine was flickering and I pressed the button.

'Hey, Cliff. You know the voice and you've got the number. Call me if you need me.'

Hank Bachelor, boy detective, still sounding cheerful. I had hours to kill before the meeting with Piper. I put my mobile on the charger and cleaned and oiled my pistol. The chamois shoulder holster was creased and dusty from hanging in a closet and I wiped it down and smoothed it out before strapping it on. It felt uncomfortable as it always had, but it sat flat and neat under my armpit and didn't sag under the weight of the gun.

The mobile was fully charged and I put it down alongside my keys and wandered through the house. I turned the computer on and checked the email, but there were no further unsourced messages and those that came up I scarcely registered. The phone rang and I snatched up the upstairs extension.

'Hardy, this is Inspector Carmichael. No doubt you've heard about Master.'

'I've heard.'

'I want to talk to you.'

'I don't know anything about it.'

'I still need to talk to you. We're on our way to your place.'

'You think I've got Stewie Master stashed away here?'

'See you directly.'

No, you won't. I snatched up the mobile and the keys and got out.

As everyone knows, time goes more quickly as you get older, but, in a funny way, when you're trying to kill time it slows down. I was still much too early for the Marrickville appointment, even after filling the car with petrol and oil and getting the tyres checked and the windscreen cleaned. If I lived in Bondi, which I'd often thought of doing, I'd put in the time at the beach, staring at the waves, but where do you go between Petersham, where I got the petrol, and Marrickville?

When Carmichael and Hammond got to my place and found me gone, the chances were they'd put out a bulletin on my car. I didn't want to drive aimlessly around. I remembered a park in Marrickville where they had some of the last remaining grass tennis courts in Sydney. As I drove I caught a news bulletin about Master's escape from Avonlea. There were still no details on how he'd managed it, but there was a full and accurate description of him. At least he wasn't described as 'dangerous'.

I parked in the shade, bought a take-away coffee across the road and strolled down to the courts. I had the mobile with me. If Stewart Master wanted to contact me and was able to, he could. Involved with an assassin, a corrupt legal and police network, an escaped convict and investigating police, my position was far from secure. I'd been in the middle of nasty games before, but not with as many serious players.

A mixed doubles match between some accomplished players was in progress on beautifully grassed courts with the white lines clearly marked. Nothing quite like it. The dinosaur era, as John McEnroe calls it, right here. The old-world aspect of the tennis game, taking me back to my teenage years playing inter-club competition on suburban grass courts, had a calming effect.

The middle-aged players all had competent serves and ground strokes, but it was clear that the surface was a novelty to them. They tried to set themselves for topspin shots but the ball wouldn't bounce high enough and they got frustrated. The players taking the net position on serve handled themselves well enough, but when it came to approaching the net at speed they faltered, unsure of their footing. All but one of them were fundamentally back court players anyway, and the woman who was most comfortable at the net chopped her opponents up severely. She and her partner were clearly going to win and consequently were having the most fun. I sipped coffee and watched, envying them the freedom to play games. I clapped one of her cross-court volleys, got an appreciative wave in reply, and went back to the car.

The mobile chirped and I answered it.

'Hardy.'

'This is Carmichael, Hardy. You're being foolish.'

I cut him off.

Marrickville has been through as many changes as most places in the inner-west. Jeff Fenech was known as the 'Marrickville Mauler', so I guess the Maltese must have had a foothold.

Then there was a heavy Greek and Lebanese presence and more recently Asians have moved in strongly. The Demetrios restaurant was a product of that earlier migrant wave, battling bravely against the rising tide of Vietnamese restaurants and Chinese supermarkets. I parked at a short distance in spaces provided for rail travellers and made my way back to the main street. I wore a loose cotton jacket with a denim shirt, drill slacks and leather boots. The Smith & Wesson rode high and tight under my arm. My wallet was zipped into a pocket in the jacket. I was sweating under a high sun in a clear sky. When I thought about it, Black Andy Piper was one of the last people in Sydney I'd want to see.

They were waiting for me at the door of the Demetrios—both big, both in suits, both ex-coppers. Who else would Piper employ and what else could men like that do once their warrant cards had been surrendered or, more likely, taken from them? I half recognised one of them but couldn't recall his name; didn't know the other.

'Gidday, Hardy, you arsehole. Remember me?'

'Remind me.'

'Loomis.'

'Oh, yeah. Mr Loomis, detective sergeant that was.'

'Right. Come this way, Hardy, and don't give us any trouble. This is a respectable place.'

There were a number of responses I could have made but I resisted the impulse. Loomis was a thug I'd run into years before when a missing person case had crossed wires with a semi-illegal police sting. Loomis liked hurting people then and probably still did. No point in antagonising him now. I followed him and the other one into the restaurant and straight down the corridor that led to the toilets. Loomis's mate held the door open and I went in with Loomis following.

'Strip, Hardy,' Loomis said, 'and then bend over.'

I took the .38 and pointed it at the bridge of Loomis's big-pored nose. 'I'll strip,' I said. 'I know you have to be sure I'm not wired. But I'm not going to spread my bum for you or anyone else and you can tell Black Andy that for me. I'm feeling fucking humiliated enough just talking to him.'

The other heavy made a move towards me but I kept the gun steady on Loomis, who gave a buck-toothed smile, causing me to remember his nickname. He gestured to his mate to back off. 'You always had some balls, Hardy, I'll give you that. You can put the gun within reach and strip. Me and Chris'll just admire your physique while you show us there's no wire.'

'Fair enough, Bucky.'

His face darkened but he wasn't about to be put off his stride. 'You'll keep, Hardy. You'll unload the gun before we go back in and drop the bullets into a pocket of your jacket. Then I think Mr Piper'll be happy to see you. Of course, if you're wearing a wire Chris and me will have to take steps here and now.'

I put the pistol on the shelf in front of the mirror between two washbasins and took off my jacket and shirt along with the holster. I undid my belt and dropped my strides. I lowered my underpants to my knees, then I pulled them up along with the pants. I lifted one leg after the other onto the shelf, unzipped the boots and pulled them off, then put them back on. It was all demeaning and tiring and made my blood boil, but I kept my eyes on Loomis while making sure the pistol was within reach.

About halfway through the procedure the door to the toilet swung in, but Chris put his weight against it.

'Not now,' he said.

Loomis, who'd been leaning against a stall door, pushed off. 'Okay. That's fine. Get dressed and we'll go and have some lunch. Remember what I said about the gun. You can hang on to the pocket knife and the mobile.'

I took my time about getting ready just to annoy him. We went back into the corridor and I flipped out the magazine of the .38 and spilled shells into my hand. Loomis leaned down to do a count and nodded as I put the pistol back in the holster. Then he gripped my wrist, twisted it and caught the shells as they fell out.

'Fuck you, Hardy,' he said.

There was a scattering of diners in the restaurant but they took no notice of the three of us as we walked towards a table at the back, half partitioned off from the rest of the place. Black Andy Piper sat alone at the table and I'd scarcely have recognised him. Never tall, he'd expanded to twice the bulk he'd had when he kicked the shit out of me at the Cross. The hair was now silvery white. With his nutcracker nose and jaw structure and leathery skin, he looked like an inflated Bob Hawke. The table was big enough for four but Piper waved his minions away and gestured for me to sit opposite him. He exchanged nods with Loomis before dismissing him.

'You're looking well, Hardy,' he said, and his growl wasn't unlike Hawke's either.

'Thanks.'

'What d'you do? Take vitamins?'

'Good genes.'

He had a glass in front of him and another beside it and there was a bottle in an ice bucket on a stand. He lifted the bottle out and showed it to me.

'Retsina?'

'Fine.'

He poured me a glass and pushed it across, topped up his own and proposed a toast. 'To letting bygones be bygones.'

I raised my glass in response. 'For now at least.'

'Fair enough. So you're still mates with that cunt Parker. He saved your bacon a few times as I recall.'

The retsina was cold and strong and I wanted to gulp it, forced myself not to. 'We're mates. Save the abuse, Piper. You've got no time for Frank and it's mutual.'

Piper took a good pull on his wine and gave a contented sigh. 'I've ordered. Tucker'll be here in a while. I love this kind of food. Mary introduced me to it. You like it?'

'Yes. Let's get down to it. Warren North. You want him for your reasons and I want him for mine. Where is he?'

Piper smiled showing teeth he'd spent a lot of money on—crowns, ceramic in front where he once had gold. 'Jesus, Hardy, not so fast. We have to come to terms. I dunno where the fuck he is but I'm going to find out. He's in control of some merchandise but he's lost the franchise, if you know what I mean. I have to know how you stand on that.'

'I couldn't give a shit. If people want to put poppy juice in their veins, I say let 'em. I'd legalise it.'

'Would you now? That'd really fuck things up. Okay . . . ah, here's the food.'

I knew I was going to have to put up with Piper's Godfather routine and decided I might as well enjoy it. The spread that was laid out looked to be enough for four or six and must have accounted for his weight gain. He speared things from a number of plates, piled them up in front of him and gave the food his full attention. I followed suit, taking about a quarter of what he did. It was the usual— stuffed olives and vine leaves, various dips, flat bread, spiced and skewered meats, grilled and pickled vegetables. Hog heaven.

I started to speak but Piper held up one hand to check me and concentrated on his food until he felt fuelled enough to get down to business. He wasn't finished by a long shot, but he was prepared to pick now and talk between bites and sips.

'I suppose you know by now how the Master thing was supposed to work,' Piper said. 'Of course, I was just a . . . facilitator, not a player.'

'I've got a pretty good idea. But North was playing his own game. I'm betting the original shipment was meant to be soft but North and maybe Master changed it to hard and that made a certain amount of killing worthwhile.'

Piper sucked on an olive, spat the pip accurately into a dish and nodded. 'Something like that. North's a ratbag and the word is he's closed down a lot of his options.'

'So, can you find him?'

'Yeah, given time. He'll be trying to cut a deal with one scumbag or another, but he's going to find it hard. Eventually he'll end up between a rock and a hard place. Do you know that Jack Nicholson's the first person to go on the record as saying that? It was when all that Polanski shit was going down.'

'I didn't know you were a movie buff.'

'I'm not. Mary is.'

'Ah, Mary.'

'That's right. Mary. You can see that I've got interests to protect in this thing.'

'One of them being Jack the Odd.'

'You've got the idea. So I have to proceed cautiously and make sure it all comes out right in the end.'

'Me too.'

'What's in it for you, Hardy? The woman? Are you fucking her? I wouldn't if I was you. That Master's a tough cunt and now that he's out and about . . .'

I'd had enough to eat but I thought about another piece of bread with some babaganoush and decided why not? It gave me a chance to think of a reply. I ate the bread in two bites and drank some retsina. 'Professional pride.'

Piper's white-toothed grin was mostly a sneer. 'Oh, yeah, I remember you were always big on that, like fuck you were.'

'Come on, Piper. You know what I want—to be there at the time and make sure the woman's safe. What do you want, apart from a clean slate for all of your mates?'

Piper slid a last piece of meat to the end of a skewer and popped it into his mouth. He chewed and then pointed the sharp end of the skewer at me. 'A hundred grand,' he said.

24

As I walked back to my car with the bullets for the .38 loose in my pocket, I thought that Piper's demand for money was a good thing. If he'd offered to help out of the goodness of his heart I wouldn't have trusted him an inch. But a hundred thousand tax free made sense. He had my mobile number and I had a number he said would reach him. I was digesting the meal and reloading the gun as I sat in the car. It suddenly hit me how suspicious this would look to an observer and brought home to me that the car itself was a hot item.

I drove to the garage in Surry Hills where I have it serviced and booked it in for a thorough check-up, telling them I'd be out of town for a while and to take their time. I hired a Mitsubishi 4WD because you never know where you're likely to have to go in this business, and drove to my office. I circled the area carefully a couple of times making sure the police hadn't posted a lookout and also checking that Black Andy hadn't given me a tail. In all likelihood, Carmichael and Hammond had gone there after Glebe and then just put out a call on the car. They'd have other things to attend to, but the murders and the escape of my client's husband and the whereabouts of the client herself would put the matter high on their list. They'd keep checking and O'Connor would only be able to keep the lid on her disappearance for so long. I'd made this point to Piper and he'd just nodded indifferently as he detached something from his renovated molars with a toothpick.

I parked at a one hour meter in William Street and went up to the office. I seldom carry the pistol but it was a comfort as I mounted the stairs in the half light, all the stairwell gets in the afternoon. I didn't expect trouble here, and that's exactly when you should be ready for it. I could hear some of my fellow tenants going about their businesses, legit and semi-legit. Stephanie Stargazer bailed me up as I put my key in the door.

'Ho, Cliff. A bad karma day?'

'Why d'you say that, Steff?'

'You look tense. Give me your details and I'll lay it all out for you, free of charge.'

For years I've resisted giving her the stuff about the time and circumstances of my birth, most of which I don't know anyway. I could get them easily enough from my sister, who flirted with this bullshit years ago and got the drum from our mother before she died. But Mum would have made it up if she'd felt like it, and from the way she drank it was unlikely she'd have remembered accurately. Dad, in the way of dads in those days, was absent from the event.

'Steff,' I said, 'When I'm less tense I'll give you all the dope you need. Right now, I'm going in to deal with my problems and play "My Sweet Lord" and burn some incense for poor old George.'

'He died happy.'

'Ten years too early. Look at Paul and Ringo. They gave up smoking, like me.'

Steff did a stylish turn of her ninety plus kilos in her purple kaftan with the mirrors in the skirt and jingled her bracelets. 'You're a hopeless case.'

'You love me, though.'

'I'll do a reading on that. See you, Cliff.'

I opened the door to the familiar musty smell. Once, the mail used to be brought up and dropped through the slot. Not now, and I'd forgotten to check the box downstairs. The answering machine was blinking so there was a message. But the bug was still in place. Did it matter?

The first message was a harmless one from a would-be client who'd have to wait. The second was from my daughter Megan to tell me she was touring with a theatre company in Queensland and was just saying hello. That was her second hello in a year. Our relationship was warming up. The last was from Carmichael, as I'd suspected. It was just to let me know that I was in trouble. I already knew that.

I unscrewed the handset the way Hank Bachelor had, and removed the device. I had no idea how the monitoring worked, but I imagined that it took sophisticated equipment at a listening post. Warren North, aka Frank Eastman aka Phil West, had more to worry about now than my phone calls. The more I thought about it the more difficult his situation looked. He'd miscalculated if he thought holding Lorrie would scare me off, and if he thought it'd control Master he'd made an even worse mistake. By now he must know that Master was on the loose and angry. The plan for getting the heroin into the gaol system was shot. I hoped North was under enough stress to impair his judgement and not enough to cause him to wipe the slate clean.

I phoned Bryce O'Connor and got his secretary. She was the person I'd bullied before and when I told her my name she gave me his mobile number.

'He said he was anxious to hear from you.'

'That's nice. Did he say where he'd be?'

Her tone indicated that she was less than happy. 'I think he was going to Mrs Master's home or her office.'

Good. O'Connor was on the job. I dialled the mobile number. It rang for a long time before he answered. That didn't worry me. Maybe he disliked the device as much as I did and fumbled with it, hoping the ringing would stop.

'Yes?'

The voice was recognisably his, but only just.

'O'Connor, this is Hardy.'

'Ah, Hardy. Yes. Good.'

'We need to talk. Where are you?'

'At home.'

'Your office said you were at Mrs Master's office or her house.'

'Ah, I was. Now I'm at home. Yes, we need to talk.'

'What's wrong? Are you drunk? Did the police give you a hard time?'

'. . . I have had a drink or two. The police? No, not so bad. You'd better come here, Hardy.'

'Where's here?'

'My flat . . . apartment.'

He rattled off an address in Kirribilli. A trip over the bridge or through the tunnel in late afternoon traffic wasn't something to look forward to, but O'Connor sounded rattled and I needed him to be able to function when the moment to raise the money came. *If* it came. I told him I'd be there as soon as possible and hung up. One good thing about the shabbiness and smell of my office is that, while I'm usually glad to get there to deal with business, I'm never sorry to leave it.

The other side of the harbour wasn't my stamping ground and it wouldn't hurt to be there while Carmichael and Hammond were on the lookout for me. Given what Frank had said, I thought I'd want to contact them when the time was right. But not yet.

The Mitsubishi handled well and I decided to take the bridge for old time's sake and because I haven't yet sorted out the options at the tunnel exit. The traffic was thick but it flowed well and I was across in that semi-foreign land sooner than I expected. I worked my way through to the address O'Connor had given me and it wasn't really Kirribilli at all but North Sydney. Why do they do it? To be able to say they live in the same suburb as the Prime Minister? That'd be enough to keep me away.

The four level apartment block was set in a garden that would have looked better a few months back, before the big dry. It was still pretty enough, with carefully tended native trees and shrubs and white stone paths with a couple of judiciously placed benches giving a nice harbour view. I could see the blue sheen of a swimming pool through the obligatory fence. The lucky well-heeled residents would be paying top dollar for every plant, bench, tile and litre of water. Security, too. An underground garage could only be accessed by remote control. To get through the gate set in a high wall that was sure to be electronically monitored, you had to stand where a camera, well up out of reach and protected by a heavy grill, could count the hairs in your nose. I buzzed O'Connor's flat—number two.

His voice came over the intercom, flat and slurred. He was on the piss all right.

'Hardy . . . Come.'

The gate swung in and I went up a path to the main door where I went through it all again. Then it was along a carpeted passage, past some enlarged photographs of the building itself and the views it commanded from different angles, to the door of number two. Quite a stroll. These weren't your little one-bedroom numbers. For the first time the thought occurred to me that O'Connor might have a family. Why else would you need an apartment this size? But then I couldn't imagine kids growing up in a place like this, pool or no pool. It had the dead feel of too much money and not enough life. It was status living and super secure. Just right in the age of the War against Terror.

I ignored the bell, guessing that it probably chimed something soothing inside, and knocked hard on the door. Even before it opened I had the feeling that things weren't right. A man like O'Connor doesn't take half the day off, go home and start drinking. Not unless something has really shaken him to the core. He wouldn't have enjoyed the interview with the police or having to run interference for Lorrie, but it shouldn't break him.

But there he was, opening the door, collar and tie in place, suit trousers, polished shoes. His hair was a bit awry and he was paler than when I'd last seen him, but there was no smell of booze and no glass in his hand. He stepped aside without a word and I went in. The small reception area gave way to a large living room with all the right fixings—bookshelves, entertainment unit, expensive furniture and a wall that was all window with a view that took in part of the bridge and went all the way across the water to the Opera House. Picture postcard plus.

O'Connor stood in the middle of the room as if it wasn't his place at all and he didn't belong there.

'What's the matter with you?' I said. 'You're acting like a zombie.'

'Nothing. Nothing. You said we have to talk.'

He was clenching and unclenching one fist and trying not to look at me. Drawing closer I realised he was sweating.

'You're in a bad way. Are you diabetic? You look like you're having a hypo.'

'No, I'm not diabetic. I'm all right.'

'You don't look it or sound it. I need you to be on the ball as this thing goes along. Who's your doctor?'

'He doesn't a need a doctor, Hardy. And you need to stand quite still just where you are.'

Stewart Master stepped into the room and the pistol he held was pointed at my chest.

25

THIS was no Kevin Simmonds, barefoot in tattered cardigan and trousers being hunted like a wild animal; not your average escapee getting pissed in the first pub or captured in the first brothel he got to. Stewart Henry Master was clean-shaven and neatly dressed in a navy tracksuit and Nike sneakers. He was sober, alert and fit-looking, as if he'd just done a good gym session, had a shower, an espresso with two sugars.

'How the hell did you do it?' I said.

'With a lot of help from my friends.' He nodded at O'Connor. 'Bryce, I want you to open Hardy's jacket, left side and take out the gun he's got tucked away in there. You gave it just a little twitch when you were on camera, Hardy.'

O'Connor, who'd relaxed a bit since the immediate cause of his high anxiety had been resolved, shook his head. 'I detest firearms. I'm not going near one.'

'I'll save you the trouble.' Moving very slowly I held the jacket open with my left hand and eased the .38 from the holster with the thumb and forefinger of my right. Still holding it like that by the butt, I flipped it onto one of the leather armchairs.

Stewart nodded approvingly. 'Very smart.' He moved smoothly across to the chair, picked up the pistol and put it in the pocket of his tracksuit top.

'We can do without the guns, Stewart,' I said. 'Nobody needs to get shot here.'

'Get this straight, Hardy. I know you're a tough guy and a risk-taker and a smooth talker and all that shit. I heard a few stories about you on the inside. But right now and for the immediate future, I say what happens down to the last detail, and you and Bryce have fuck-all input. Understood?'

O'Connor was nodding vigorously but I wasn't prepared to give Stewart the total control he wanted. I ignored the gun he still held and moved a few steps to lower myself onto the arm of a chair. 'It's a nice speech. We know you're good at that. There's no evidence you're any bloody good at anything else except escaping from prison, and that's got a limited application.'

'What the fuck are you talking about?'

'I'm talking about your wife being held by a desperate man who's already killed three people that we know of, and what can be done to save her life.'

It took a little of the starch out of him. He must have been running on adrenaline since sometime before his escape and that fuel only lasts so long. His compact body seemed to sag a little and he blinked a few times, a sure sign of fatigue.

'I'm working on it,' I said. 'She's my client and I feel responsible, but that's a responsibility we share. You wouldn't have done what you've done without thinking you could help her. Escaping'll add years to your sentence. You must know that.'

Master appeared to lose interest in the pistol. He lowered it and brought his other hand up to his face, massaging a spot between his eyes. I guessed he had a throbbing headache.

'We have to pool resources,' I said. 'I need to know what you know. You're whacked. I reckon you're safe here, at least for a while. I suggest you put down the guns and let Bryce get us something to drink and something for your headache. Then we talk and see if we can help Lorrie.'

He wavered. 'I don't know.'

'Fuck you and your "I'm the boss" bullshit. See how close I am now? I reckon I could get to you before you could shoot me, because I'd know when I was going to move and you wouldn't.'

'What about Bryce?'

'Bryce'll do whatever we tell him. Won't you, Bryce?'

O'Connor did some more nodding.

Master put his pistol on the coffee table, took mine out of his pocket and placed it there too. A metallic clink. 'I've never shot anyone and I don't want to start now,' he said. 'Unless I have to for Lorrie's sake.'

We men of action treated O'Connor like a servant, getting him to bring us drinks and warning him to stay away from doors and windows and phones. At that point I decided I was wrong about O'Connor perhaps having been a professional footballer. I reckoned that if he'd played the game at all, it would only have been at his private school. What I'd taken for force and aggression now seemed more like bluff backed up by status and money and support staff. When Master had bailed him up after he'd left Lorrie's office, it appeared he'd gone straight to water and had done everything he'd been told.

'Where'd you get the gun?' I asked.

'The same place I got the clothes and the walking around money. Don't worry about it. You say you're working on finding Lorrie. Tell me. I've got some ideas. Maybe they fit together.'

I told him everything about the meeting with Black Andy Piper and the money. No reason not to. O'Connor brought in whisky, ice, soda and glasses. Master stared at the whisky longingly.

'Beer,' he said.

O'Connor produced two Crown Lagers. Master opened one and drank sparingly. 'Been off it a while,' he said. 'The hard stuff'd knock me flat the way I feel.'

O'Connor poured himself a large scotch. 'As your legal adviser, I—'

'Shut up,' Master snapped. 'I'm still not sure you weren't in on the fucking set-up.'

I mixed a weak scotch and soda with ice. 'I don't think he was. He probably knew something was queer before things went very far but he didn't do anything about it.'

'I deny it,' O'Connor said.

Master drank a little more beer. 'You probably wouldn't have the guts. Okay, Hardy. Do you reckon Piper's fair dinkum and can he do anything?'

'Yes and yes. I wouldn't say that except for the money he wants.'

'How were you planning to get hold of that?'

I pointed at O'Connor, who almost spilled his drink.

Master nodded. 'Good thinking.'

'Impossible,' O'Connor said. 'That amount of money. Every bank transaction over ten thousand is—'

'Don't be naïve, Bryce. I know people who'll advance you

that in cash in return for certain assurances, and Hardy does
as well, probably.'

'Yeah,' I said. 'I can think of a couple who'd advance him,
not me.'

O'Connor slumped back deflated in his chair. The
thought of being still further involved in this mess took away
his brief flash of professional spirit. He undid his top shirt
button, loosened his tie and worked on his triple scotch.

'You said you had some ideas,' I said to Master. 'When
you heard Lorrie had been taken you decided to get out. So
you must have thought you could do something about it.'

'That's right. First off, I checked on the kids. Britt seems
to have that under control.'

'For now,' I said. 'Also Lorrie's office. I reckon that Fiona
knows how to keep the lid on things. But the cops won't stop
asking questions about her and something'll break pretty
soon. That'll put pressure on North. Black Andy's my only
hope. What about you?'

He turned the bottle around in his hands before tilting
it up and taking another drink. The sinews were stretched
tight in his throat and the easy movement of his arm under-
lined his fitness and flexibility. Master had demonstrated
through his criminal life and just now that violence
wasn't his thing, but he'd be very dangerous indeed if it ever
became his thing, and perhaps that time was getting close.

He was a long time making up his mind. He had a lot to
think about, primarily who to trust. It all depended on how
well he was functioning. I turned to O'Connor. 'Brew up
some coffee. Make it strong. And have you got any pep pills?
You know, stuff to take to keep you awake when you're
working into the early hours on your clients' behalf?'

He looked at me as though I was mad.

'Nodoze,' I said. 'Dynamos. Caffeine tablets, for Christ's sake.'

'Guarana.'

I'd tried them. No effect whatever, but better than nothing. 'Get some and give them to him with the coffee.'

Master gave me a grateful look and seemed to decide to speak. 'Hardy, I don't know . . .'

Then my mobile rang and we both jerked like stringed puppets. I pulled it from my pocket and flipped it open.

'Hardy.'

'Carmichael. We know your car is in for work in Surry Hills and that you're driving a white Mitsubishi licence number WPC 832 with a red stripe on the bonnet and a roof rack. We've got a chopper up looking for Master and you're on the list. We'll find you. Be sensible.'

I cut the call.

'What?' Master said.

'The cops, tracking me. O'Connor!'

He poked his head around the corner. 'What? The coffee's nearly ready.'

'Put it in a thermos. Where did the police interview you?'

'At my office. Why?'

'They'll search every location for every person involved. We have to get out of here.'

26

'Not me,' O'Connor yelped. 'I'm not going anywhere with you two lunatics.'

'Yes you are, Bryce,' Master said. His tiredness seemed to be in remission. 'You're going to climb back into your suit and get your briefcase and all the stuff that says how important you are and come with us.'

O'Connor mustered up a last shred of courage. 'Or?'

'Don't try me, mate. Like Hardy says, I'm looking at life to nothing. It'd make no difference if I killed you.'

'You wouldn't.'

'I might. That's your worry. I just might.'

'This is insane. Let the police come. Tell them everything. They'll find this North character and your wife and—'

'He'll just give in, will he and cop a few murder charges? No way, I know him and others like him. He'll clean the decks.'

'You can't be sure.'

'Can't be sure of anything. Suppose it worked out like that. I was part of a police intelligence operation that went wrong, was probably fucking bound to go wrong. You think those guys are going to own up and let me walk away? No chance. If I go back inside I'm dead.'

'We're wasting time,' I said. 'Get the coffee and the pills and the scotch. Put them in your briefcase and anything else that shows how much money you've got. We're out of here.'

We did it quickly. Master scooped up the guns and I let him. O'Connor showed good housekeeping skills and we were out of the apartment within minutes.

'Where's your car?' I asked O'Connor.

'In the garage.'

'We'll take it and put mine down there.'

Another few minutes, a couple of zaps of the remote control, and we were on the road in O'Connor's silver grey Beemer with the Mitsubishi safely tucked away from eyes in the sky and on the ground.

O'Connor was driving with me beside him and Master in the back, and as soon as we turned out of his street he asked where we were going.

'Good question,' I said. 'Master?'

'Other side,' he grunted.

'Tunnel or bridge?' O'Connor said.

'Whatever you fuckin' please.'

He sounded ragged again and I opened O'Connor's briefcase, ignoring his protest, and took out the thermos and packet of herbal kick-starters. I passed them back to Master. 'You have to get a grip. You were about to tell us something back there when my phone interrupted you.'

Master accepted the thermos and I heard him screw the top off and pour. The BMW held the road like a snake slithering on glass. I heard him break the tablets out of the foil, drink and swallow, drink again, and replace the thermos cap.

'Fuck, that was strong. I've changed my mind, Hardy. How do you get in touch with Piper?'

'I've got a number to ring.'

'Do it!'

'Oh shit,' O'Connor whispered.

'What?' Master and I spoke simultaneously.

'I'm almost out of petrol. I wasn't expecting to go touring around with—'

'Shut up!' Master sounded more alert and focused already. Maybe my metabolism's wrong for Guarana. 'This is your territory. Where's the nearest service station?'

'I don't know. I fuel up where I park. In the city.'

'Fuckin' yuppies,' Master said. 'Hardy?'

'I'm inner-west. This is downtown Baghdad to me.'

O'Connor's fleshy pink knuckles were whitening on the wheel. I looked at the gauge and saw that it was dipping below empty.

'There!' Master snapped. 'Pull in at that BP.' He was suddenly fully charged and I had to wonder how many of the pills he'd taken, or if they were what O'Connor said they were, and just how strong O'Connor had brewed the coffee, or what else he might have put in it. Then I heard the slide on Master's pistol as he cocked it.

'While he's getting the gas, Hardy, you make that call.'

O'Connor slotted the car in to a pump, got out and looked helplessly at the mechanism.

'He doesn't know what to do,' I said to Master. 'And I'm not sure my mobile's going to operate in here with all this shit around. We're going to attract attention. I'm going to help him and then make the call. Okay?'

There was a silence that felt like a minute but was probably only seconds. 'All right, Hardy. You pay. He gets straight back in. I almost trust you. But I'll blow your fucking brains out if you . . . shit, I feel weird . . .'

I got out of the car with the hair on the back of my head bristling, thinking that Master could snap at any minute. I helped O'Connor unhook the pump and get the petrol flowing.

'What did you put in the coffee?' I muttered as we bent over the hose.

'Nothing.'

'The pills, then?'

He sniggered. 'Rohypnol in a Guarana box. It'll jazz him up for a while and then he'll be flat on his face.'

'You're a sneaky bastard.'

'I'm a lawyer. It's expected.'

I glanced at the car. Master was staring suspiciously at us and his eyes had a fixed, haunted look. I flipped open the mobile phone and felt in my jacket pocket for the napkin with Piper's number.

'Who's this?' Not Piper's voice.

'Cliff Hardy for Andy Piper.'

'Hang on.'

Piper's gravelly growl came on the line. 'What the fuck d'you want, Hardy?'

I had to think quickly. Was a phone Piper used likely to be bugged? Probably not. How would he react to what I had to tell him? With luck, it'd shake him up a bit. 'I've talked with Stewart Master. He's armed and he's angry and he's hopped up on something. I had to tell him about our deal.'

'Fuck you!'

'He's all right about it. Wait a minute.' O'Connor was looking helpless as the pump clicked off. I waved him back to the car and put the pump back on the stand.

'Hardy,' O'Connor muttered. 'This is our chance. Come on. You're a business person, a professional, not an antisocial criminal like him.'

I hesitated but only for a split second. O'Connor was for self-preservation at any cost and I've never been that way. I snarled at him to get back in the car and he did.

When I had the phone back to my ear Piper was spluttering.

'Don't tell me to wait, you cunt.'

'Shut up and listen. The shit's hit the fan. The cops are looking for me and I've more or less kidnapped Master's lawyer. Master's got some sort of idea about where his wife might be but he's holding off until I come up with something. If you've found out anything at all, tell me. I need to string him along.'

I heard him shout at someone to turn a race call down and then he came back on the line. 'I still get the hundred thousand.'

'If it works out, yes. Come on.'

'It's not much, and it might be more to do with the shipment than this cunt North, but there's some connection. I'm hearing about a guy named Starcevich and his flash boat.'

'And?'

'That's it.'

'That's not worth a hundred grand.'

'It's not bad for a couple of hours and it fucking better be worth it.'

He hung up. Black Andy at his best. I put the phone away, checked the amount on the pump and went in to pay. We'd been there too long with too big a chance of attracting attention. I hurried back to the car to find O'Connor sitting white-faced behind the wheel and Master swearing at him and waving his gun around.

'Get started, O'Connor. Knock it off, Master. D'you want everybody around to take a second and third look at you?'

O'Connor got the car moving and Master subsided. His mood swings were impossible to anticipate and getting more violent. One minute he was in control, then he was ranting. He was quiet for a short spell and then he said, 'Well, what did you learn?'

'Does the name Starcevich mean anything to you?'

I heard the upholstery hiss as he slumped back against the seat and I turned around. 'Jesus Christ,' he said. 'I know it.'

I twisted back to make sure O'Connor was headed for the bridge before turning again to look at Master. He was a mess; the drug was working on him but he was fighting it with everything he had.

'I don't know where North lives or what boltholes he might have,' Master said slowly, battling to keep from slurring. 'But I do know someone who's involved in getting the shipment to where it's supposed to go and I know that North and he are friends, as much as anyone could be a friend to a prick like him. That's Ray Starcevich.'

'If you knew that, why didn't you go straight for him?'

'I did. He's got a boat at the Watsons Bay marina. I went there but they said he was out on the water. Then Bryce here convinced me you were on the ball and that it'd be worth my while to see you first. Fuck knows that it has been.'

I thought about it as we approached the bridge. Boats had figured generally in this bloody business from the start—Reg Penny's yacht, the drug shipment coming by boat, Lorrie mentioning that she had a yacht. For no good reason I said, 'That's where Lorrie's boat is.'

Master's tired head jerked. 'What? Lorrie hasn't got a boat.'

'She told me she has and you didn't know about it. It's called the . . . some kind of red wine . . .'

'Jesus,' Master said. His pale eyes, red-rimmed now from fatigue and stress, went hard. 'You've seen it? You've been on it . . . with her?'

I kept my eyes steady on his and a fist ready to fire in case he lost it completely. 'Don't be stupid. No. She just mentioned it early on, when I was getting the picture about you and her and all this.'

'What does all this babble mean?' O'Connor said as he slowed to join the traffic selecting lanes.

'It means we're headed for Watsons Bay,' I said. 'So make sure you get in the right lane.'

The marina and yacht club were located to the south of Camp Cove, putting them close to Vaucluse. That might have made it more expensive but around here it hardly mattered— a coffee could cost five bucks. O'Connor knew the way because he'd been there earlier in the day with Master when he failed to find Starcevich. Master had fallen quiet in the back and O'Connor was gaining in confidence by the minute.

'He's falling asleep,' O'Connor whispered. 'If I drive around for a few minute—'

'Don't even think it.' Master could hardly say the words; it wasn't much of a threat.

The marina had three jetties about twenty-five metres apart with moorings on both sides of each. The daylight was beginning to fade and most of the activity was of the pack-up-and-go kind. Boats again, I thought. I was beginning to hate the bloody things. 'Where was Starcevich's boat supposed to be?'

'Jetty one,' Master mumbled. '*Ballina Belle.*'

'Have some more coffee and try to stay with it,' I said. 'I'm going to check something out.'

'What the fuck's wrong with me?'

'O'Connor drugged you. Don't hurt him unless you have to, just keep him here. Back in a minute.'

I got out and walked towards the marina office searching my memory for the name of Lorrie's boat. *Yalumba*? *Penfold*? Then it came to me—*Merlot*. The woman in the office looked about ready to call it a day but there were still a few people moving around. I had no idea what security was like at a marina, but I didn't see any high gates or electronic equipment.

'Excuse me, is Mrs Master's yacht, the *Merlot*, around?'

'Around? What do you mean around?'

'I'm sorry, I'm not familiar with boatspeak. Is it here?'

She pointed to jetty three. '*She's* moored there.'

'The thing is, Mrs Master's thinking of selling it. I've got her lawyer here, a Mr O'Connor and the prospective buyer. I wonder if we could take a look at her?'

Suddenly her level of interest went up ten notches. 'That poor woman. I helped her learn to sail. She caught on quick. Then there was that trial. I read all about it.' She snapped her fingers. 'O'Connor. That's the name of the guy who defended her hubby, right?'

I nodded. 'Right.'

'I saw a photo of him. Fatty. He's here?'

I pointed back to the BMW.

'He didn't do such a flash job. I'm surprised she has him as her lawyer.'

I shrugged. 'They get their claws in. Can we look at the . . . yacht?'

'I guess so.'

There was one more bridge to cross. 'Thanks. I suppose you've been busy, nice day like this, long weekend coming up?'

'Flat tacked. Haven't lifted my head.'

So with any luck she didn't know about Master's escape. 'Okay. Thank you. We'll go and take a look.'

She tapped her watch. 'I'm off in a few minutes. I'll tell the night guy.'

'Don't bother,' I said. 'We won't be long.'

I went back to the car, opened the rear door and helped Master to sit up. I relieved him of the guns and he didn't protest. 'You're going to have to make an effort, Stewie,' I said. 'Just a short walk and then you can lie down and sleep and with any luck you'll be safe.'

His pupils were pinpricks and his pulse was racing. I opened O'Connor's briefcase, retrieved his mobile phone and handed it to him. Then O'Connor and I got Master on his feet and moving. Luckily, he was light and even two-thirds spaced he was coordinated enough to make it possible for two big men to support him.

'What're we doing?' O'Connor hissed.

'We're getting him onto Lorrie's boat. When we reach the office you give the woman in there a smile. She knows you.'

He did it and we manoeuvred Master along the jetty and down onto the deck of the *Merlot*. I used the picks attached to my Swiss army knife to pick the lock on the door leading to the boat's saloon. Master was almost out to it by the time we got him comfortable. I could feel O'Connor getting ready to be the super-professional again and that was the last thing I wanted.

'Take off his shoes,' I said.

'What?'

'You heard. Do it.'

Doing the menial task deflated him a bit, especially as he made a mess of it.

'Right,' I said. 'This is the way I see it. You've harboured an escaped criminal, driven him and drugged him. Your prints'll be all over the packet, and what you could be doing with a supply of the date-rape drug I hate to think. Your reputation's about to take a nose-dive.'

'You can't be serious.'

'I'm very serious. I can put you deep in the shit or keep you out of it altogether. It's up to you.'

'W-what do you want me to do?'

'Simple. Just stay here with Master until I contact you.'

'How long will that be?'

'Hard to say. If Starcevich's not there it'll be a matter of minutes. If he is it'll be longer.'

'What're you going to do?'

I looked at Master lying stretched out on the seat in the saloon. His eyes were closed and his features had relaxed and he was breathing easily, innocent as a trout in a pool. In my estimation he'd handled himself pretty well through all this so far and might have continued to do so but for O'Connor's intervention. Out of prison, with appropriate clothes, money and a gun, he'd had a lot of options, but he'd chosen to check on his kids and try to help his wife. I thought about the sterility and heartlessness of Avonlea and didn't want to be a party to putting him back there if I could help it.

I had two pistols and I felt like throwing them overboard. Master's, I certainly would. 'What would you expect?' I said to O'Connor. 'You reckon I'm going to go over there with guns blazing?'

O'Connor nodded.

'Forget it. I'm doing what you wanted me to do all along. I'm calling the police.'

27

I CROSSED on a pontoon that ran between the jetties and squinted in the gloom at the boats lined up along jetty one. They were all shapes and sizes but mostly big. A few people were still on board tidying away or preparing for tomorrow's sail or whatever boaties do last thing. The *Ballina Belle* was one of the biggest—a long, two masted white thing that made Reg Penny's boat look like a bathtub and the *Merlot* look very modest. I took up a position about thirty metres away, protected by a high-riding catamaran.

Show yourselves, I pleaded silently.

On cue, a man appeared from below with a bucket attached to a rope. He dropped the bucket into the water and hauled it up. He was big, bearded and dark, not Warren North. He handled the full bucket carefully, watching to make sure none of the water splashed on the deck. Couldn't have that.

North's appearance a few seconds later registered with me almost as a physical shock. Even at that distance and in that light he was recognisable from the photograph, and his movements were those of the gunman I'd glimpsed briefly— smooth, fluid. The two men spoke, then North stepped over the side and onto the jetty. That put paid to my plan to get the police. Had I ever really meant to play it that way or was I just comforting O'Connor? It wasn't an option now with North on the move. He walked purposefully towards the entrance to the marina and I fell in discreetly behind him, moving across to the next jetty as soon as I could. He appeared relaxed and confident and I didn't like the look of things. If he'd managed to work the situation out to his own advantage somehow, Lorrie was no longer of any value to him.

I gained on him, walking quietly, with traffic noise from the road above helping. It was dark in the section of the car park he was approaching and he pulled keys from his pocket as he neared a new-looking Volvo station wagon. He worked the remote and released the door. I didn't have time to consider. I charged him, head down, and slammed the door into him. He was totally off guard and collapsed, hitting his head twice as he went down. He was unconscious and bleeding from a wound above his ear. I crouched in the shelter of the car and felt his pulse. Strong. I used my Swiss army knife to cut his T-shirt from his body and then used the strongest parts of it to strap his feet together and bind his hands behind his back. I tore a thin, well-stitched strip, and gagged him with it, pushing some of the material into his mouth. Not enough to choke him, but enough to keep him quiet. I bundled him into the back and collapsed the back seat rest onto him.

There was a packet of tissues on the front seat and I used one to prevent leaving a print as I opened the glove box. His pistol with the silencer detached sat there under a much-thumbed *UBD*. I closed the glove box and walked away, leaving the keys on the bonnet.

Things were quieter but not yet still at the marina and I strode in, giving a confident signal to the night watchman. 'A quick word with Ray Starcevich.'

He nodded and I went back along the jetty towards the *Ballina Belle*. I didn't know how much time I had so there was no room for subtlety. I stepped over the side and approached the steps leading below. 'Ray,' I said. 'You there?'

Maybe he was expecting someone, maybe I sounded a little like North, but he climbed the steps and I waited until he was almost at the top before I jumped out and kicked him in the crotch. He tumbled down the steps and I went down after him with my .38 in my hand and ready to punch or kick again if I had to. There was no need. Starcevich lay groaning at the bottom of the steps with his arm twisted at an impossible angle. He tried to lever himself up using both hands and screamed with pain.

'Who the fuck're you? Where's Warren?'

'Warren's out of the picture. Where is she?'

I had the gun hard in his groin and I was very calm and he was very afraid. He jerked his head towards a short passageway.

'In there.'

'Show me.'

'I can't walk, you cunt.'

I jabbed hard. 'Crawl.'

That's what he did for a couple of metres before he managed to lever himself up and stagger to a cabin door. He was big and strong and although he was in pain he was still dangerous.

'Lie down,' I said.

'What?'

'Lie down!'

He looked at me and then at the gun and lowered himself into the narrow space. I rested my foot lightly on the crook of his damaged arm. 'You give me any trouble and I'll fuck it completely. Likely you'd lose it. Understand.'

He nodded and I opened the cabin door. Lorrie Master lay on a bunk with plastic restraints tying her to the frame at the wrists and ankles. Some sort of ball with strings attached had been forced into her mouth and tied around her head. Her eyes were wide open and she looked at me as if I was some kind of apparition, a stress-induced fantasy.

'It's okay, Lorrie,' I said.

I turned back to Starcevich. 'If I go in there to get her loose, do you think you could get away before I could shoot you?'

'No.'

'D'you want to get out of this alive?'

'Yes.'

'You've got a chance. Just a chance. Lie perfectly still and your chances go up.'

I felt him flop and took away the pressure. I stepped into the cabin and used the shorter, sharper blade to cut Lorrie free. She used her hands to remove the gag.

'Oh, Cliff. How—?'

'There's no time. Can you walk?'

She eased herself upright and groaned. I flashed a quick look at Starcevich. Still compliant.

Lorrie stretched and massaged her leg muscles. 'I think so. I wasn't trussed up like that all the time.'

'Okay. You have to go up and go across to your boat.'

'Jesus, are we . . .?'

'Yes. Coincidence. Just go across quietly and say I'll be contacting them in a minute.'

'Who?'

'No names. Just go, Lorrie. I've got business with this guy.'

She was dressed in the clothes Fiona had bought her and wouldn't look out of place. She scrambled to her feet and glanced down at Starcevich.

'He wasn't too bad, Cliff. It was the other one.'

'Good. He's in luck then. Go!'

She blew me a kiss and took off. I gave her time to get there and then called O'Connor's mobile.

'Hardy?'

'Right. No names. How is he?'

'Coming around. Couldn't have taken more than one. Either that or he's got a high tolerance.'

'Good. I want all three of you out of there inside ten minutes. There's going to be a lot of activity. Don't argue. Take them anywhere you like, just do it.'

'But—'

'Do it. D'you want the bloody cops to find you with them?'

'God, no.'

I cut the call and turned my attention back to Starcevich, who'd lifted himself up into a sitting position, cradling his arm and awkwardly massaging his crotch. I'd forgotten about the kick and was almost sympathetic. 'She put in a good word for you or I'd be inclined to give you a very hard time.'

'You've done enough, you cunt. Me arm's broken for sure and my balls're—'

'Spare me. Tell you what I'm going to do. I'm going to give you, let's say twenty minutes, before I phone Black Andy Piper and tell him where you are.'

He tried for indifference but terrified alarm won.

'If you can cast off, or whatever you call it, and get the engine started and steer with one wing, you should be all right. But cops're going to be here first and then Andy, and I don't know . . . Up to you.'

He had some guts. He pushed back and slid up against the wall until he was on his feet. 'You're that prick Warren was worried about—Hardy.'

'No names, Ray. Better get going.'

I retreated to the steps, climbed them and left the boat. Master's pistol went into the water with barely a splash. I looked towards the car park and saw brake lights come on and off and headlights swing away in roughly the spot where we'd left the BMW. I walked along the jetty and heard an engine surge into life behind me.

I went through the gate. The car park was almost empty and the Volvo was lying quietly in the shadow of a tree with no other car parked close. I walked up a path away from the car park and found a public phone where I rang Carmichael's number. If he checked back on the source of the call, that's all he'd get. Then I moved a bit higher and to the left, further away, and sat on a bench.

The *Ballina Belle* had pulled away from the jetty and was headed out into the dark water of the harbour. Two cars approached the marina. One cruised the car park while the other stood off at a distance. When they were satisfied, Carmichael and Hammond got out of the first car, drew their weapons and approached the Volvo. Then it was lights, camera, action. More vehicles streamed down into the car park and the officers of the law went into their practised routines. They sealed the area, talked to the night guy at the marina and the few other boaties still around, walked along the three jetties, but they paid no attention to me up on the hill.

I watched them pull North from the Volvo, untie and de-gag him and transfer him to a car. Carmichael, wearing gloves, took the pistol and silencer from the glove box and put them in a paper bag. Contrary to popular opinion, cops don't always take items away from the scene of a crime in plastic bags. Sometimes they use paper. I don't know why. Maybe it's special paper, less contaminating. I'd have to ask Frank Parker.

My mobile rang several times during the operation and I saw Carmichael vent his frustration on his underlings each time, but I didn't answer. Eventually they all left and the Watsons Bay marina settled back for its night time sleep with the lapping waves and the straining ropes and the groaning timbers. To hell with it. I never liked sailing and liked it still less after all this.

When all was quiet, I phoned Piper.

'The woman's safe. You'll get your money.'

'Fuck the money. Where's Starcevich?'

'Last I saw him he was pointing his boat out into the harbour. Probably going for the Heads.'

'You arsehole. He's got the H.'

I couldn't help laughing. 'That's your problem, Andy, not mine. I'll be in touch about the hundred grand. I know it's not much . . . but you probably still want it anyway.'

There was some satisfaction in that. If Black Andy had masterminded the whole thing, seeing himself as the Napoleon of Sydney crime now and into the future Master had sketched, he'd run into a few obstacles. I didn't know where Starcevich would take the stuff and I didn't care. The amount he was carrying was a spit in the ocean compared with the worldwide trade, and while the politicians and preachers stay as blind gutless on the subject as they are now, the trade'll flourish.

I eased myself stiffly off the bench and began to walk aimlessly, wanting a drink and vaguely thinking of a taxi. I had two cars, both miles away and not available. Then I smelled food and heard laughter and the clink of glasses. Stimulated, I started to think a bit more clearly and had an idea. I used the mobile phone again.

'Hank? This is Cliff Hardy. You busy? Good. Meet me in the beer garden of the Watsons Bay Hotel and I'll buy you a drink and tell you a story.'

28

'BUT what I don't understand is why you put them in the boat,' Hank Bachelor said. 'Why not just leave them in the car while you did the business?'

'Hell, give me a break. I was making it up as I went along. Maybe I had some romantic idea of her and him, him and her, sailing away into the sunset. I don't know.'

We were in the beer garden eating fish and chips and drinking Cascade. I mean I was drinking. I'd had three or four and didn't feel like stopping.

Hank was going more slowly and eating more. 'Anyways, I'm glad you called me. This is cool.' He pointed to the restaurant at the end of the pier. 'I was never here before. What's that place like?'

'Great but expensive. I'll take you there when you finish the course. You should bring Pammy.'

'Hah. Pammy's a vegan and she doesn't drink.'

'I don't see a big future for your relationship.'

'Why did you call me, Cliff?'

I lifted the cold bottle to my mouth and took a long drink. The beer was smooth and the taste felt good and pure after all the things I'd been doing and thinking over the past few hours. 'I dunno,' I said. 'I suppose I trust you and I suppose I had no one else to tell the story to and I know I need a lift home.'

He laughed and I joined him.

We sat quietly for a while and ate and drank while the people around us did the same. It was one of those rare moments when I felt in tune with other citizens. It was partly alcohol-induced and wouldn't last, but I enjoyed it. Under the stars at Watsons Bay within sound of the water and in good company wasn't a bad place to be and the empty feeling that came with the finish of a case hadn't yet cut in. I wrapped up the leavings of the meal and dumped them in a bin and I told Hank I was going for another beer.

'You're drunk,' he said.

'Right. One more to seal it. Then you can drive me home.'

'Sit. I'll get it.'

He came back with a beer for me and coffee for himself. 'You said you trusted me. How about the lawyer?'

'Don't trust him but I've got a lot on him and he knows it. Client–lawyer confidentiality gives him a fair bit of protection. It'll work out.'

'The cops'll put you through the wringer.'

I took in some more beer. Still tasted good. I shrugged. I think I shrugged. 'Won't be the first time. They've got their killer all wrapped up. They'll be happy.'

'They haven't got you-know-who.'

'Won't be the first time. Won't be the last.'

'I guess.'

I finished the beer and heaved myself upright. 'Tell you one thing, Henry. Are you a Henry-type Hank, Hank?'

'Howard.'

'Tell you one thing, Howard. If you put any of this in one of your essays you better be sure to change the bloody names.'

Bryce O'Connor, true to lawyer form and with a lot at stake, handled things well. He hid Master somewhere and Lorrie went back to her office and home without any serious alarm ever being raised. O'Connor and I managed the delivery of the hundred thousand to one of Black Andy Piper's 'associates'. There was no escaping that obligation. I asked the guy we met whether they'd caught up with Ray Starcevich and he didn't reply. I never found out.

Carmichael and Hammond grilled me as I knew they would. They were sure I was involved in the capture of Warren North, and they suspected me of being in contact with Master at the very least, but they had no proof. They threatened me with obstruction and conspiracy but the threats were empty.

They were happy to have someone to charge over the murders of Fay Lewis and Jarrod Montefiore and possibly Reg Penny. To their own satisfaction, they could close the book on these cases. But, given what I'd told them about North's shadowy connections and what they'd learned themselves, they could be under no illusions. Bringing him to trial would be a long process and securing a conviction would be hard going.

Strings must have been pulled between Canberra and Sydney, the feds and the state cops and God knows who else, because when Stewart Henry Master surrendered to the authorities, his sentence was reduced to five years to be served in a minimum security institution. Terrorism and the whipped-up threat of it dominated the headlines and Master's progress received minimal publicity. The word is he'll be out on day release before too long.

I've tried to steer clear of cases involving undercover police operations and the intelligence services. With those people you never know when you've got hold of the right end of the stick. Master looked set to get off lightly. Did that mean there really was a legitimate undercover operation and he was bound to come out smelling cleanish? Or had he undertaken to be the heroin conduit from the start and just got lucky? Black Andy Piper's fingers were in so many pies it was impossible to tell where his influence stopped and started. Was North his man all along? I never found out and maybe they didn't really know themselves.

Lorrie Master was happy to fork over the hundred grand. All in all, she'd outlaid more than she'd said she would when she engaged me in the beginning but she didn't complain. She invited me to sail with her, but Stephanie Geller cast my horoscope and said I shouldn't venture out on water, especially given my gypsy ancestry. Anyway, by then I had other things on hand and I didn't go.